PRAISE FOR IGLOO

I had my fingers crossed for Nirvana's happiness from the first chapter until the last. A swiftly paced adventure and a true romance to melt your heart in winter. Had to stop myself booking an alpine lodge holiday immediately after reading.

– Shirley McMillan, author of *A Good Hiding*, *Every Sparrow Falling* and *The Unknowns*.

Treat yourself to this sparkling Christmas love story and escape to the snow-clad pine forests of the Alps. Jen Burkinshaw gives us witty, warm and charming Niv and Jean-Lou to root for – perfect for romance fans of all ages.

– Anna Mainwaring, author of *Tulip Taylor* and *Rebel with a Cupcake*.

Igloo is a heart-warming story of first love set against the stunning backdrop of the French Alps. I was rooting for Niv and her journey from the start! Nirvana is such an inspiration to girls – particularly given the current market – for standing up for what she believes in. A girl who is passionate about joinery and can make an igloo from scratch? And make her own love story happen at the same time? Go Niv!

– Eve Chancellor, poet and author of short stories on *East of the Web*.

Needs to be in everyone's Christmas stocking

Full of humour, delightfully fresh phrases, and surprises, *Igloo* is a perfect YA Christmas read. We are in Nirvana's mindset immediately and we're rooting for her to become what she is destined to be. The dialogue is funny, sparky and exciting between the two main characters, and their differences in interests and character are a perfect balance. I really loved the atmosphere of this book, from its language and locations to its heart. I'll be reading more by Jennifer Burkinshaw.

– Ruth Estevez, author of *Meeting Coty*, *The Monster Belt*, *Erosion*, *Jiddy Vardy* and *Jiddy Vardy High Tide*.

Igloo is a superb novel. I was totally involved in Nirvana's story and had to read it to the end. Now I'm quite sorry I've finished. The main characters are totally believable and intriguingly complex; the supporting cast all beautifully realised, from little Claude to the horrendous Ghislaine. The debate over Niv's future is extremely well reasoned on both sides. The descriptive writing is amazing too. I wanted to visit that igloo myself!

– Bob Stone, author of *Letting the Stars Go*, *The Custodian of Stories* and the Beat trilogy.

A cosy, curl-up Christmas read with a hot chocolate and all the toppings!

What a lovely story! Such a gentle romance with enough edge so that it's not saccharine and cliché but also with not too much edge that it makes it hard to read or has triggers! This is something that is often hard to find in YA fiction. The teenage voice was great – enough naivety balanced with a little stroppiness and hot-headedness. Nirvana has a passion for carpentry and now for Jean-Lou. Most of all, I wanted to know if they make it!

Determined to follow her dreams, Nirvana quietly grows in strength in this well-paced, evocatively set coming-of-age novel that genuinely made me smile.

– Carole Estelle, *The Reading Jackdaw*, book blogger

IGLOO

Jennifer Burkinshaw

I do hope you enjoy Nirvana's story.

Jennifer Burkinshaw

Beaten Track
www.beatentrackpublishing.com

Igloo
First published 2022 by Beaten Track Publishing
Copyright © 2022 Jennifer Burkinshaw

Paperback: 978 1 78645 556 7
eBook: 978 1 78645 557 4

Cover Design: Debbie McGowan

Beaten Track Publishing,
Burscough, Lancashire.
www.beatentrackpublishing.com

For my beloved Mum
(1935 – 2021)

'igloo' –
a refuge for rebels,
an escape from parents

(definitions according to Nirvana Green)

PART 1:
24 DECEMBER

ONE

I FLING MY SKIS down on the snow.

"Have a good lesson, love!" Mum says.

"Find someone to speak French with, *Nirvan-ah!*" Dominique says, in full French stepmum mode as she fixes me with her ice-blue, husky-dog eyes.

"Enjoy *débutants*, Niv!" Claude crows over his shoulder as our mums sweep him off to the intermediate group. Barely four years old, but true to form, he's mastered basic skiing in two days.

I won't! I singsong in my head to each command. *Not a hope of me enjoying this afternoon.*

Which, if they thought about me for even one second, they'd realise.

A thick curtain of snow closes behind them. I raise my eyes out of this murky valley; somewhere up there are the Alps I'm longing to see, the mountains Grandad's waiting to hear all about. My dream of a white Christmas is the kind where the snow actually stops, revealing frosted pine forests and toothy crests under blue skies and a tangerine sun.

Little children start to gather nearby, waiting for our instructor, Moustache, nicknamed by Claude and me for obvious reasons. He's late again, thankfully.

I scowl down at my stiff, plastic ski boots. Am I really gonna clamp myself to two metal strips just to slide down a bit of ice, on repeat, the only view the back of the kid in front of me, for two long hours?

But ski lessons are expensive, a pesky voice in my head reminds me.

Yep, but I didn't ask for more school, more timetables, ski uniform or even this surprise holiday that means I've had to abandon all my plans.

But now my little brother's no longer around to keep tabs on me; if I can cut real school, I can sure as heck cut ski school.

This is *my* Christmas Eve too!

As I clap my skis together over my shoulder, they feel less heavy than when I carried them down from the chalet and over the road. And now, even with the ridiculous weight of my boots and the weird heel-toe walk their rigidity forces you into, I'm starting to feel…lighter.

I dump my skis and the helmet from hell at the wooden racks next to the only restaurant in the village. My heart as well as my head is lighter now, lighter the further I get from the gaudy plan of all the pistes and ski pulls scarring this poor, invisible mountain, free from the trappings, literally, of skiing.

As I CLUMP my way along the ice rink of a car park, I have to watch my every step.

A pair of black snow boots appear bang in front of my toes.

I look up.

4

The woman blocking my way is glaring into me from dead, expressionless eyes, all the more striking because the rest of her face is beautiful—creamy skin and full lips.

"*Attention!*" she snarls, lips actually curling. "*Imbécile!*"

What the actual…? My mouth drops open as my brain scrambles for a response.

"You don't…You're the…" My heart pounding furiously, words fail me in English as well as French.

I can see the second she realises I'm English: the scorn on her face multiplies by the hugest possible factor. My head shakes in a sort of involuntary shudder at this hateful woman. Gotta get away from her, pronto. I take a heavy step to my left and pound on as quickly as my boots on ice will let me.

Mrs. Angry-Pants, Claude would call her and cut her down to size, but she's nothing as simple as that. I've never seen such *spite* in a face *and* directed at me. More eager than ever now to escape the little resort and get rid of the bitter taste she's left in my mouth, I trudge on past the 'blue' piste towards the edge of the village and a track I glimpsed when we drove in two days ago, signposted *Route Forestière*. I'm determined to get to the forest itself.

And maybe, if I'm really lucky, a view. Three days in and I've yet to clap eyes on a mountain!

My heart gives a little flutter: the track ahead of me untrodden, draped with soft, smooth white, which squeaks underfoot as if in protest. Being the first, though, soon turns out to be a slog in these boots, but I refuse to be held back by them, even when it gets to the point of heaving myself up deep snow, step by heavy step.

5

An uphill struggle is how it's felt for months now, ever since I started veering away from the Niv that Mum and Dominique want me to be. I've had to learn the hard way not to let *anyone* stop me doing what *I* really want, especially when my parents banned the thing that means the most to me. Which is why, so far, it's had to be a secret, that application form hidden away on my laptop, poised to *send* before the end of the year. I'm reaching out for a future that fits me, no matter what *they* think. But time's running out now: I've gotta tell Mum my plans before we get home.

And she's not going to like it. One little bit.

I'm sweating under all my layers as the tips of tall, red markers poking out of the snow now guide me left, back towards the village. The calls of ghostly skiers reach me, and I must be getting near the top of the drag lift, as I can hear the clunk of metal on metal of the drag poles.

And finally, as the route elbows back away from the village again, the edge of a pine forest! Below this point, many of the trees have been felled for ski runs. But here, white arms reach out to me in welcome, their deep sleeves so different from the bared-branched silver birches of my happy space at home, my secret workplace in the woods.

The Grove is where I can be my real self, creating something that will really matter. Four days ago, it was glittering with medallions of lightly frosted leaves between pewter trunks, and it's where I expected to be for most of the Christmas holidays, hanging out with my best friend Sab. But then Dominique announced this surprise ski trip as her Christmas present.

Now, as I step towards the friendly pines, the falling flakes are lighter and drier like feathers tickling my cheeks.

And what's that, tucked right into the side of the path so it's almost in the wood itself?

I laugh out loud. It is. It really is. Curving up out of the snow...

An igloo!

I'VE NEVER SEEN a real one before.

Its builder has picked a good site—level, with the hope of a panorama from its stubby tunnel, yet still camouflaged till you're right on top of it. Sheltered by the trees, it's also not far from where the piste basher shoves the excess snow into a low wall that is a great source of compacted bricks.

Exactly where I'd have built one.

Intrigued to see how it's been made, I stride towards it. There's no sign of anyone having been here recently. No footprints other than mine. Maybe kids were on a ski holiday, like me, then had to abandon it. I skim my hand over its snow-clad roof, loving its soft roundedness after the straight metals of skis, poles, lift tugs.

I take my gloves off to pull out my phone; Sab'd love to see this. Stepping back, I try to capture the igloo and its entrance in the middle, with the pines waving behind. But no signal here: I'll have to send it from the chalet later.

On my knees now, I peek into the tunnel. The aqua-tinged light and pure, dry smell make me smile all over again. Dragging my boots behind me, I crawl inside.

ONCE I'VE TURNED to face front, I sit upright, my legs straight in front of me.

At once, I'm in a soundproofed cocoon, the world on pause. The snow-whirling wind, clatter of skiing, the fog-grey are left far behind. Here, all is still, calm and clear. And it's amazingly warm for an icehouse! But then, of course, that's why the Inuit build them. I sweep a layer of flakes off my hair.

Tipping my head back, I inspect the dome. Despite the heavy snow out there, brighter edges define each of the bricks. That says to me they don't meet as tightly as they could—I might redo them at some point.

I hug myself: another time I've followed *my* instincts instead of any supposed grown-up's agenda and found something amazing! Here I am, inside but outside. Or the other way around. And utterly private. I close my eyes, taking in my igloo's fresh smell, its silence, its secrecy.

At last, a space just for me.

A place to be free.

"Er... bonjour?"

TWO

ARE YOU KIDDING *me?! Is nowhere sacred?*

My eyes open to meet a pair of brown ones between a Roman nose and a black beanie. Their head and shoulders are sticking into *my* space. Those eyes shift up to my hair, and my hands follow, trying to hide it— as if I could.

"*Bonjour,*" I huff.

Now what?

"This," he continues in French, casting a glance around the dome, "this is *my* igloo."

His igloo?

My brain scrambles for the French to say, *Then drag me out cos I really like it in here!*

And isn't there some rule about squatters' rights and possession?

But not even four years of sharing Claude's bilingual upbringing help with this situation! I rehearse some French words I *can* find in my head and clear my throat.

"You can't own an igloo. Unless it's in your own garden."

His eyebrows rise; he looks more amused than convinced.

"I built it," he counters.

I glance upward. "The roof could be better."

9

A dimple pings in his right cheek. "Yet it's lasted three weeks already. Since the first snow."

Unlike the blur of sounds since we arrived in France, his French has separate words, so I can understand quite easily.

"Oh! Then you live in the village?" And my own French seems to be flowing fine now, without Dominique on my shoulder.

"*Ba oui*. Jean-Louis Jaboulay. Seventeen," he adds.

A jolly-sounding name! I sniff. He looks at me expectantly.

"Nirvana Green, on holiday, sixteen."

"Nirvana!" His mouth shrugs, mock-impressed. And unlike Dominique, he gets the emphasis in the right place. "What a name!"

"Yep" I sigh, "Too much." *Ultimate Bliss*, it means. Mum clearly had no idea what I'd turn into.

We look at each other. Stalemate.

I bite my lip. "Er, if you...er..." I nod towards the entrance to suggest he retreats. "I'll go." Maybe I'll have to build an igloo of my own next time.

"Perhaps..." he starts.

I wait.

"Perhaps...you want to share, Nirvana?"

I look into the space next to me. It's only a small igloo, no more than his stride, I'd say.

Everything Mum's always drilled into me about being alone with strangers in remote places runs through my head. I twist my mouth to one side, follow my instinct. "Maybe just for a few minutes."

GIVEN HE HAS half the space I had to turn in and he's a fair bit bigger than me, it takes an awkward manoeuvre for him to get in and face forward. Now he's the one who gets to stretch out his legs, also in padded trousers but walking boots rather than plastic ski boots. His legs are so long, his feet are almost at the entrance.

He removes his hat and shakes off the snow between us, revealing very dark, slightly wavy hair—far more restful than my 'maple-leaf magenta' as Grandad calls it, like my nana's. Mum says people pay good money to have the hair shade I'm stuck with.

As he turns to me, I catch a trace of outdoors, the mountains. "So, Nirvana, why do you need an igloo?"

Sounds like an interview for igloo rights! And *need* one? But I get what he means: even though I didn't know it was going to be here, it was—*is*—exactly what I needed.

I point to my boots. "I'm avoiding my ski lesson." The simpler answer.

His dimple deepens. "I don't like skiing either."

"But you live in a ski resort!"

"I can ski. Most French children have to learn. But far too much hassle for me."

"Me too!" I agree. I've always loved being outdoors but to see my surroundings, never sport for the sake of it. "But my parents insist on it. So, you'll understand, why I need this igloo to escape it."

He nods, still smiling.

"And you? Why did you build this igloo?" *Since you live locally,* I think.

11

"This imperfect igloo?" he teases whilst rifling inside his padded jacket and extracting a paperback, which he brandishes like a magician. "For reading."

His tone implies this is the most obvious place for it—some sort of minuscule outside-inside library. His book cover features a mediaeval-looking guy with a ruff, a beard and a black hat.

Essais de Michel de Montaigne

"You know this philosopher?" he asks.

Who's he kidding? As if I'd know any philosophers! That familiar feeling creeps in, of inferiority, being on the outside of things I should know.

Then I remember. "No, but I know Ruskin. He was an English philosopher and painter."

It's because of my Art GCSE unit on Ruskin that I'm so eager to see the mountains, including Mont Blanc and the glaciers he drew so vividly.

"I don't know any English philosophers," he says, "because I study German instead of English. So, it's really lucky you speak French!"

My heart grows. For the first time ever, I'm not ashamed of my French. Even though I'll never sound like Claude, without it, we wouldn't be speaking at all. And when I don't get something quite right, he manages to find a natural way to say it back to me as it should be.

"Ruskin," I start, trying to find the words, "he thought beauty is for everyone, and…essential?"

"*Essentielle, oui*," he confirms.

"What *is* the philosophy of Montaigne, then?" I ask him.

"He's got loads of themes. In the essay I've just read…"

I find I'm watching his lips as his French, soft and light, dances off them. His dimple operates like a punctuation mark, flickering every time he likes what he's talking about.

"...Montaigne says, 'When I walk alone in the beautiful orchard, I bring my thoughts always back to the orchard, to the sweetness of it... When I dance, I dance. When I sleep, I sleep.'"

Sounds like this Montaigne lad, from way back when, was ahead of the mindfulness wave. Dead easy in an orchard, anyway.

I smile at him over the top of his paperback. "When we're in the igloo, we bring our thoughts always back to the igloo."

"Exactly, Nirvana," he says, putting his book back in his pocket.

He uses my name pretty often, I notice. And I'm finding I like my name better than I ever have, feel less like insisting he calls me *Niv* instead. But I feel shy, for some reason, about using his.

I close my eyes again and try to refocus my mind on the igloo. It's no longer silent because of the soft breathing of this lad— *Jean-Louis*—right next to me.

Yet somehow, I've still got more room than since we arrived in the Alps.

Yikes! How long did I zone out? I don't want to overstay my welcome, but when I open my eyes, Jean-Louis smiles at me. He *is* very smiley in general. Upbeat.

"I should go," I say reluctantly. "Ski school'll be finishing soon, and my parents will be meeting me."

He shoves his hat back on.

13

"Does it ever stop snowing here?" I ask him as we stand for a moment in front of the igloo, gazing into the murkiness. "I came up hoping for a view of the mountains."

"Of course it stops! Tonight, the skies will be clear, I promise you."

I catch my breath. "For Christmas Eve night."

He opens his mouth, hesitates, opens it again.

"If you can come back later, Nirvana, I could introduce the mountains to you."

He says it as if they are his old friends. I bite my bottom lip to rein in a smile.

"What time?" I ask.

THREE

THE BEST PART of skiing, whether or not you've actually done any, has to be the *après-ski*. For a start, all the torturous ski stuff's well and truly out of sight and mind—in the drying room under the chalet. Then there's tonight, the mountains and Jean-Louis!

Inside, we're all in our merriest Christmas moods, having done exactly what we wanted with our afternoon. And I did, after all, find someone to speak lots of French with, not only during my ski lesson, but later too!

From the luxury of my double bed, I report back to Sab, starting with my igloo pic.

NIV: Instead of skiing, chillin…

She's already typing. I can just see her, propped up against her headboard. A complete movie buff—anything and everything—she'll be watching some film on her laptop while her parents think she's working.

SAB: Co-el! Well built!

My fingers hesitate. But I can't take the credit.

NIV: It was already there actually.

SAB: Uh-oh! Beware Goldilocks situation.

I laugh at one of her trademark comparisons. I swear Sab has a sixth sense, though she credits her freaky ability to read people and situations from observing behaviour in movies. That's *why* she watches them, she says, and it really does seem to explain why she's so good at marketing her family's business.

NIV: No bears – just a local lad.

Now she pauses! Half of me wishes I could take it back, save our chance meeting from the Sab microscope.

SAB: Hot? Even in the cold?

NIV: S'not like that. Gonna show me the mountains when skies clear tonight. Shh!

SAB: Right, so, note to self: secret, starlit tryst NOT a date.

Whoa! I groan. Now I know I've been too free with my phone thumbs. Everything about Sab is sharp—eyes, nose, elbows—but particularly this extra sense. She'd fit right in at MI5. Even though she can't read my body language and voice, her mind'll be working overtime on every little thing I write—or *don't* write.

NIV: No biggie – cept, fingers crossed, the view!

But lads *are* A BIG THING when you go to an all-girls' school. Just less so for me, as I've encountered a fair

16

few in my bunch of Saturday jobs and more recently at Hackspace. Some are fun to do woodwork with; a few have asked me out. I've never met anyone like Jean-Louis before, though, and anyway, he's waaay out of my league. Tonight is just him showing me 'his corner', as the French put it. And I can't wait for eleven o'clock!

SAB: Sneaking out?

She knows full well my parents wouldn't allow me out at night to meet someone they've never met. Which is a bit of a shame because I think they'd find Jean-Louis pretty interesting—as well as a great source of French conversation practice!

I open my window and lean out to photo how my bedroom opens onto a balcony that runs around the corner of the chalet to the outside steps. Then I send it as my answer to Sab, with the caption: **My escape route**.

SAB: More à la Juliet than Great Escape!

I laugh: we watched this war classic together after she'd asked my grandad for his fave film and admired the ingenious ways the prisoners of war tried to escape *their* guards. I've only got one attempt, though, and it has to come off!

Time to shift Sab away from talking about me.

NIV: What you doing tonight?

SAB: Revising Eng Lit.

Working on Christmas Eve? Just for a sec, I forgot she and her family don't celebrate Christmas, and even if they did, she'd probably still have to revise. It's a toss-up who's worse between her dad and Dominique, who constantly treats me like one of her failing pupils. Our families can't seem to accept that Sab and I are just not the high-flyers they wish we were—except in films and woodwork, which no one seems to appreciate.

> SAB: *Aka watching the Romeo and Juliet movie.*

Aha!

> **NIV: And French Speaking and Listening for me! See ya – got to go light the log burner.**

I really do, that's my job.

MOUTH-WATERING SMELLS OF garlic waft down the hall from the kitchen as Dominique starts the cheese fondue—a first for us kids. She's making a special meal tonight for *le réveillon de Noël,* which the French generally celebrate more than Christmas Day. In our case, it's gonna mean mountains of cheese, chocolate and cream— all things Dominique usually strictly rations! *What will Jean-Louis be eating with his family tonight?* I wonder.

As I pass the bathroom, it sounds like elephant's wash time as Mum tries to contain Claude's excitement for tomorrow. In the lounge, I light up the Christmas tree that came with the chalet. The aromatic pine smell is delicious, but it's such a shame it's been cut from its roots. At home, I dig ours up every 20th December and replant it twelve days later. Though our family presents are under this tree, there's no Rova wriggling her way among them and no Grandad for the big opening session tomorrow. Tough when it's the first after Nana. He said he was fine going to my uncle's, doing something different from usual, but then he always tells Mum what she wants to hear.

Now for the log burner, something I've been campaigning for at home. I arrange some pinecones in the base and put a match to them. Once the blue flame fans into gold, I add some slim logs. I gaze around the room, lit only by the golds of the flickering fire and tree lights. It really *is* a Christmassy chalet, honey pine from ceiling to floor, warm under my socks.

At the patio doors, I leave the wooden shutters open to keep an eye on the snow, still falling like someone's tipping it directly from the roof. Will it really stop later on? Jean-Louis seemed so sure. Oh God! What if it doesn't? Should I still go to meet him? We didn't talk about that. Gazing in the general direction of the igloo, I have to admit to myself, I'd still be going in a blizzard!

As we DIP all our bread chunks on long forks into the cheesy pot and the three of them rave about skiing, part of me wishes I could tell them about *my* brilliant afternoon. But another part of me knows it'd lead not only to lectures but increased surveillance on the pistes.

"How will Father Christmas fit down that pipe?" Claude asks as we polish off a cream-filled French version of chocolate log for afters. He means the narrow flue of the log stove. I distract him by hanging our stockings by the patio doors to keep *Pere Noël's* options open. I can't stop smiling when I peer out and see in the blaze of light on the balcony that while the flakes are still falling, they're only half-hearted about it now.

The time starts to drag once Claude's in bed. I have to shake Mum awake. She's snoring softly, with an empty wine glass resting on her tummy, but she and Dominique need to be fast asleep later if I'm to creep out. So, I talk them into a board game from the chest that comes with the chalet. I won't at all mind Dominique winning at Monopoly!

KNACKERED FROM SKIING and more wine, they head off for bed around ten. As I clean my teeth, I'm thrilled all over again to have got rid of my braces last month. And at least I can wear a hat tonight to tone down my hair.

In my bedroom, I gaze out of the window without putting the light on. And yes, just as Jean-Louis foretold! The snow, for the first time in three days, has actually *stopped*! The sky is still veiled with grey but thinly enough for the faint lemon of a crescent moon to show itself. My tummy flutters happily.

Leaving my shutters open, I roll into the middle of my double bed for a bit. I switch on the porcelain bedside lamp with its own mini-chalets and stars cut out of it so it casts sweet shapes onto the golden-syrup walls and beams. Apart from a log cabin, a chalet—pine outside and in—would be my dream home.

Still half an hour to go!

As a last resort, and in some sort of solidarity with Sab, I pick up my eReader, my birthday-Christmas present combined, a top choice for a bookworm. If only I was one. Dominique downloaded my GCSE novel, *East of Eden,* so I could 'reread' it on the journey. Since our English mock's the first day back, I really do need to know how Cal's story ends. Might have happened to miss that lesson. However, I do know that Cal's the same age as Jean-Louis, poor lad, and just had a shock when he found out the mother whom he thought was dead is living in the very next town!

It makes me think again about my mystery parent.

Not that I'm daft enough to believe my dad lives near us in Lancashire or anything, but I've been thinking about him more and more since September, when Mum and Dominique put a stop to my woodwork days at Hackspace. Their aim was to make me focus on my GCSEs, but I just couldn't live without making stuff, especially when I had such an important mission.

That's where my secret times in the Grove came in, thank God. It's in my DNA, I'm convinced of it, this need to create, preferably from wood. What feels unimportant and alien to Mum feels vital and normal to me. And now I've turned sixteen, I can apply to the donor register to find out more about him. *If* I choose to.

I check my wrist. Yes! Finally! 10:31!

As I CREEP into the hall, there's not a peep from the bedroom next door. After collecting my walking boots and ski jacket from the coat hooks and bunching out the others so you can't see one's missing, I tug my ski trousers and thermal fleece over my PJs and pull on my bobble hat. Next, I carry the chair from the little desk to the window—the front door is far too noisy. I clamber onto the chair and with a clumsy and painful swivel on the window ledge manage to lower myself feet first to the balcony.

Statue-still, I strain to hear any movement from Mum and Dominique's room. Nothing must stop me now!

Finally, I exhale and reach back inside to pull the window to, careful not to let it fasten.

Now my eyes have adjusted to the dark, I almost gasp; bang opposite, the Moon is lantern-bright over a round-shouldered, gentle giant of a mountain. I follow its contours down over white forests to huge, zigzaggy moon shadows of pines cast onto the smooth, white pistes like massive cardboard cutouts on a blank canvas.

For a long moment, I stand stunned by the sheer beauty of it; at the Christmas Eve mountains.

The next bit is easier: I tiptoe along the balcony and around the corner to the side door and the steps down to the drive.

One last glance to check the front of the chalet, and I'm off!

MY BREATH MAKES cauliflower swirls in the slicing air. I pass in front of the row of apartments, keeping a sharp lookout for Jean-Louis, in case he's setting off around now too.

As I cross the road, a group spills out of the resto, all jolly after their Christmas Eve meal, their voices echoing around the valley. The village has streetlights along its one road, but once I get beyond the car park, to the forest path, the Moon lights my way. My heart leaps: here are big, fresh footprints made since it stopped snowing!

Even though it's so much easier in walking boots, I slow down as I round the last corner to the steepest part so I'm not out of breath when I reach the igloo. And now, I stop. Have to.

The moonlight's scattering spangled snow crystals all over the igloo, and just in front of it stands a tall shape.

FOUR

NOT EVEN TRYING to hide my smile, I make towards him, standing there as if he's responsible for this achingly extravagant display of beauty all around us.

"What a night, Jean-Louis," I tell him, shaking my head in disbelief. Truly, I've never seen such a sight.

His smile's just as big. "Hi, Nirvana."

I move to stand alongside him. At last, my view: matte-black outlines against a glittering, deep-purple sky.

And all completely

still

and

silent.

Only for us.

"So, the mountains?" he says eventually. "Directly opposite, meet Mont Ouzon."

This wide, scalloped mountain looms behind our chalet, its silhouette clearly outlined as if in black marker.

Jean-Louis adds a massively complex French number involving *mille* and several *cents*, which must be its height, but I get a bit lost and give up.

"So, very high then," I say.

"You can see Lac Leman from the summit."

Lake Geneva. Makes it seem so near, but it took us an hour and a half to drive from there to here.

"On our left," Jean-Louis's arm swings to point to a narrower, craggier mountain, "is le Roc d'Enfer."

I shiver at the curved hook of the rock of hell. I wouldn't like to get too close to him. *It.*

"And over there"—to our sharp right—"Mont de Grange."

This gorgeous triangle of white-chocolate Toblerone, a story book mountain, makes my heart soar. A path starting from the village cuts through a magical pine wood, promising to lead you all the way to its peak.

I turn towards Jean-Louis. "It looks like you could walk to it from here."

He shakes his head. "It's at least ten kilometres beyond the wood and impassable. Sorry, Nirvana," he adds, as if he'd make it reachable if he could.

Now we complete our circle, the igloo is in front of us, my gentle giant of a mountain behind it.

"The best view of all is from the top of this one, La Pointe du Mont," he tells me. "From its summit, you can see Mont Blanc and the whole mountain chain."

Hoh, I breathe. "I have wanted to see Mont Blanc for age." He tilts his head. "Ever since I saw Ruskin's paintings."

"One day, you'll visit it, Nirvana."

I look up at him. He sounds so sure, but I searched for it online soon after Dominique dropped this surprise holiday on us, and it's a ninety-minute drive from here. No way am I gonna be able to drag my family away from their viewless skiing. And anyway, right now, these dramatic but kindly mountains standing all around us are more than enough. Slowly, I rotate, taking pictures from

25

all angles, even though I know no image can match being part of them in this exhilarating, piny air.

This is the best Christmas Eve ever!

I glance at my wrist: it's just after midnight.

"*Joyeux Noël*, Jean-Louis!" I exclaim.

He turns towards me. "*Joyeux Noël*, Nirvana."

We need to…I want to…I don't know. Shake hands, do that French cheek-to-cheek kissing. But the moment passes, and I wrap my arms around myself, suddenly feeling the cold.

"Shall we go inside?" I suggest.

HE PUTS A backpack I hadn't noticed before between us and produces a large jar with a pillar candle melted onto its base; puts a lighter to its wick. The golden flame casts tablets of light high up on the igloo walls. I catch my breath and look more closely at what must have been a honey jar, embossed as it is with honeycombs.

I beam at Jean-Louis through the glow. This nighttime igloo's even more exciting than this afternoon. More magic.

For a while, quite comfortable with silence, we just are.

"Have you had a special meal for Christmas Eve?" I ask him after a bit.

He shakes his head. "You?"

Slowly, with him inferring the gaps in my French, I tell him how Dominique prepared it. That involves explaining our whole family set-up—how she's Mum's wife, Claude's bio mum yet my mum carried him; Claude's and my separate donors so we're not even biologically related but how I love him at least as much as if we were.

Jean-Louis listens as if it's nothing unusual at all.

"So, will you be celebrating tomorrow—today—instead?" I ask.

He looks down at the igloo floor. "Christmas is no big thing in my family. Perhaps it is for you because of Claude?"

"No way! I'd love Christmas anyway, and not only for the presents and food."

He regards me across the candle's gleam, waiting for more, his chestnut-brown eyes framed by very black eyelashes. I don't want to sound too...quirky, but I can't change who I am.

"My grandfather and I, following the traditions of my grandfather's grandparents," I explain slowly, "also celebrate...midwinter," I finish in English. "The shortest days?"

"*Plein hiver*," he supplies.

I nod, though 'full winter' doesn't capture its beauty like one English word does.

"So Grandad and me," I carry on, "we wait for the solstice before we light up our fir trees—to welcome the sun as the days begin to get longer. And we gather green leaves to show..." Stuck with a complicated structure, I shrug and end in English, "Some things never die."

"*Certaines choses ne meurent jamais*," he says. I nod. He's guessed right, just by using context.

"My grandparents marked the turning points of the year too," Jean-Louis tells me. "They lived close to the land because they were dairy farmers high on Mont Ouzon."

I catch my breath. "Just opposite!"

"Yep. Chalet Ouzon, a small place," he tells me.

I stay quiet, giving him another chance to tell me something more about his family.

He doesn't.

"This year, of course," I say eventually, "our Christmas Day will be different."

"You'll miss your grandfather?"

I hesitate. I'm feeling heaps better about being away from home now.

"A little. As well," I screw up my face, "I've got a ski lesson tomorrow afternoon."

He looks at me. "Unless..." he starts.

My heart jumps. "Unless?"

28

FIVE

THE LIGHT SLAMS on.

Claude lands on my bed.

"He's been, Niv!" he yells. "Father Christmas did find a way in!"

"Light off!" I yell back, covering my eyes with one arm.

When I'm safely back in darkness, images of last night's mountains and Jean-Louis in our golden igloo tumble into my sleepy brain.

And previews of this afternoon, *Christmas* afternoon, back at the igloo.

But would he have suggested it if I hadn't complained about my ski lesson?

"It's after seven," Claude says pointedly, breaking through my daydreams.

I groan.

"How much after?"

"Three minutes."

But I've been in bed far too few hours! I pull the pillow over my head.

Claude lifts it off again. "Ni-iv! You promised."

And it is *Christmas!* My brain finally kicks in.

"Open the shutters then, pea-brain."

"I'm not big enough, flea-brain!"

I haul myself out of bed, open the windows and shutters, but I'd forgotten it's still dark at this time. Back to heavy, swirling snow, with a deep covering over my nighttime tracks—a good thing, or I'd have to be out there brushing them away. You wouldn't even know all those mountains existed, let alone the igloo.

But thanks to Jean-Louis, *I* know they do!

"Hurry up, Niv!" Claude says.

He's turned on my bedside light, revealing the contents of our stockings, all mixed together on the duvet. My heart twitches. This is when Rova usually rips the paper with her teeth and spits out the soggy bits.

I think of Jean-Louis again, maybe not getting many presents at all today. He said so little about his family last night, instead letting me ramble on. Did I go on too much? He's such a good listener, it's hard to tell.

Claude shoves a parcel into my hand, and soon I'm tearing stuff open too and we're jamming chocolate-orange segments sideways into our cheeks. Once everything's open, he tries to lay claim to this really lovely snow globe that must have been in my stocking, complete with mountains and glittery snow. Snow you can actually stop when you invert it, unlike the real world.

"You can have any of these, Niv," he says, laying out the other treasures.

A monster truck! Yo-yo! Maybe the slinky if the chalet wasn't all on one level.

"Tempting, but no," I tell him. "Not even instead of that nifty set of moustaches."

He picks up the card of 'taches. We both get the giggles when we see a handlebar one just like Moustache's. I attach it to Claude's upper lip.

While he goes to get dressed, I grab my phone and check out my best panorama from last night. I so badly want to send it to Grandad, but how can I without implicating him in my secret? So, it just goes to Sab, with the caption:

My date with the mountains!

Next, I bob my head around our mums' door to wish them Merry Christmas and tell them I'll take Claude to the resto this morning for pastries to give them a lie-in. I can't pretend to myself I haven't thought about running into Jean-Louis, and I'm curious to see where he lives—in one of the chalets near us or an apartment.

CLAUDE AND I are apparently the only ones foolish enough to be awake at this hour: we see no one as we wade through the deep snow of the shortcut, across to the apartments and the only shop in the village, from where we hired our skis. Here, the side road's easier to walk on.

As it joins the 'main' road through the village, we pass its frosted signpost, *Ouzon le Mont*. How I wish I could point out to Claude where Mount Ouzon is, as well as Toblerone Mountain and the path to it through the enchanting pine wood—Toblerone Wood, I'll call it, since it appears to lead right to the mountain. Will I be able to see it in daylight from the igloo this afternoon?

Finally, another person! On the other side of the road, a figure is just finishing clearing the path to the resto. As we get nearer, I can see his shoulders are slumped into the slow, heavy movements of his shovel.

"*Bon Noël*, Monsieur Gilbert!" Claude chirps, clearly knowing him from previous breakfast runs.

The man straightens up. "*Joyeux Noël*, you two," he says, his rather forlorn face transformed by a smile when he sees Claude's 'tache. "Two minutes and I'll be in to serve you."

"I'll finish it," I offer, reaching out for his shovel. Having cleared the drive outside the chalet only once, I can imagine the torment of repeating it, day after day.

He shakes his head. "Thanks anyway," he says, setting to it again.

The name of his resto is to the right of the door on a painted wooden sign—*La Wetzet*. Whatever that is, there's a sad, dead sort of feel to it.

Warm, smoky air hits us as we step inside. As we stamp our feet free of snow on the mat, my eyes travel around the pine walls of the eating area, darkened with age; the chairs are stacked on the table revealing a wooden floor that is also a tarry brown.

I follow Claude to the right, towards the bar, and the whiff of cigarettes gets increasingly strong. At the far end of the bar is a customer on a high stool. Smoking *inside*! The smell is concentrated, much worse than the outdoor wafts you sometimes get. Claude turns to look at me, his little face screwed up in confusion and disgust.

A stickler for rules, he walks towards the woman. Wearing a ski jacket, she's staring blankly down into a cup on the counter, so all we can see is her black hair. She seems not to have even registered our presence.

"Excuse me, *Madame*," Claude starts in his perfect French, looking up at the smoker from behind his moustache, "but inside, smoking is forbidden."

Forbidden, *interdit,* is an important word for Claude, to be respected, and on smoking, I'm bang with him.

She raises her face. I should have known! That cow from the car park yesterday, now taking another drag on her cig. Childish or what? Claude turns to me, his eyes wide, almost frightened.

"Mrs. Stupid Pants!" I label her, to reassure him.

Hands curling as I prepare my French, I move to stand behind him. "It's been illegal inside for over ten years now because it's dangerous for others."

She raises those eyes to me. Expressionless eyes that won't look away. I try not to be the first to break the contact, but it becomes too long, too hard. When I look aside, she sneers, actually sneers, her lip curling. She takes another long pull and blows a stream right over Claude's head at me.

I gasp. My arms are shaking now. I don't get it. Don't get her. And I'm not having it!

"You don't do that to—" I start, in English, my French failing me, but the door bangs before I get any further, and I turn, relieved to see Monsieur Gilbert coming to take his place behind the bar. He can sort out this... this bitch now.

As soon as he comes into hearing, she gives this tinkling laugh and stubs out her cigarette in her saucer.

"Busted!" she tells Monsieur. "The little *gendarme*," she nods towards Claude the policeman, "has caught me!"

Blinking in disbelief at her joking about what just happened, I look from her to Monsieur Gilbert.

He shakes his head and tuts. "Ghislaine!" he says, like she's a regular and maybe this is something that's happened before that she can't really help.

I turn and narrow my eyes at this Ghislaine—an ugly name for a woman with an ugly character. She gives me a little smirk, like she knows she's won: s'not like I can report what she's done to Monsieur Gilbert, is it? This woman, the like of which I've not met before, confirms what I already know: adults are just big teenagers, at best.

"Here you are, young man." Monsieur Gilbert puts our bag of pastries on the counter. "And, may I say, I wish I had such a moustache."

Claude, back to himself, smiles, peels off his 'tache and reaches up with it for Monsieur Gilbert. My heart grows with pride at my little brother. What a contrast to that grinch! While she's far from the first adult I've despaired of, she's by far the vilest. What IS up with her?

Determined not to let her spoil more than a few minutes of our Christmas Day, I take our breakfast, telling Monsieur we'll see him later.

As we make our way back to the chalet, hungry for breakfast and more presents, I peer through the snow all about…just in case.

But it looks like I'm gonna have to wait till this afternoon for Jean-Louis.

SIX

ONCE WE'VE BOLTED down the pastries, it's time for presents from under the tree. Most of them are Claude's, which is fair enough, especially since I've already got my eReader.

For me, a beautifully soft jumper in moss green.

"I'll wear it tonight," I tell Mum, smiling. Even *I* know my usual hoodies won't do for our Christmas dinner at the resto.

I present her and Dominique with the wood chimes I made for them from some offcuts of Grandad's oak tree, and Claude with a wooden snowman I designed, which you have to assemble yourself. Then we FaceTime with Grandad and our cousins at Uncle Graham's to open our mutual presents together. Rova muscles in on the scene as usual. Grandad's putting on a fine performance of keeping the show on the road at his first Christmas without my nana, but it doesn't convince me.

"You did this, our Niv?" He's definitely wobbly as he holds up the painting of our great oak in his garden at Oak Vista—the tree that three-year-old Niv named Querky when Grandad told me its Latin name, *Quercus*. Or so the family legend goes. But Querky had to be felled, Oak Vista about to be sold; that was eighteen months ago.

"Am I that bad at painting?" I ask Grandad, trying to lighten things.

Now he smiles, and it's my turn to wobble when I open the memory book he's put together for me, *all* at Oak Vista, where I spent the first nine years of my life, before Mum met Dominique and they bought our little terraced house together.

The album starts with a black-and-white picture of him and Nana fifty-three years ago on the day they moved into Oak Vista. Querky, already around 200 years old, must have witnessed so much over his many decades, including me chasing Rova around him as a toddler, collecting his acorns as an eight-year-old, clambering into his canopy when I was older.

That part of our lives is well and truly over—unless I do something about it.

When the call's finished, I gaze out the window and hope Jean-Louis is opening something as meaningful. But somehow, I doubt he is.

THIS AFTERNOON, AS a Christmas concession and instead of our lessons, Dominique invited Claude and me up in the chair lift with them to the top of the mountain and some harder pistes. Obviously, only I declined, meaning I get extra igloo time now Mum and Dominique don't need to be back for the end of Claude's ski lesson.

With Moustache being even later than usual, it's easy to dump my skis and helmet again and stride out as best I can for the igloo.

All the way up the track, mine are the only footprints, but it's snowing so thickly, if Jean-Louis came up even half an hour before me, you wouldn't know it. I can tell before I even get close to the igloo, though, that he's not there. If *feels* empty even from a distance.

But that's okay, Niv, I tell myself as I crawl in. *You did want the igloo to yourself, didn't you?* It's just, I'd have brought something to do if I'd known I was going to be on my own—my sketchbook or even my eReader.

Then I remember Montaigne: 'When you're in the igloo, bring your mind to the igloo'. I close my eyes and focus on my senses: the smooth cool under my bum, the almost sterile smell, the stillness and thick walls insulating me from the world outside. I've read it's possible to actually hear snow falling. I don't believe it, but breathing slowly and deeply, I try to keep my attention only on flakes falling on the dome above.

Jean-Louis must, after all, be having a good time with his family today. That's good. Isn't it? I screw up my eyes even more tightly to try to stay in the igloo. *Or is he staying away cos I nattered on so much last night, sounding like a right nut with that solstice stuff?*

A minute or so later, I give up on mindfulness and open my eyes. The interior of the igloo no longer looks as cosy and welcoming, and I don't want to be here any longer. I can't go back to the chalet; I don't have the key. Dominique, paranoid about it getting lost in the snow, has it zipped into the inner pocket of her ski jacket.

To the resto! Sab'd say. *If ever there were a hot-choc situation, this is it, Niv!*

COLD TO MY heart, I crawl my way out, unfold myself and make for the path back down.

"Nirvana!"

My heart sparks. I whip around.

"Sorry, I was delayed," he says slightly out of breath, still striding towards me. "You're leaving already?"

37

"Yes, no. No," I repeat, to be absolutely clear, although I *was* leaving. I'm not anymore!

"Merry Christmas again," he says, grinning.

"Merry Christmas," I tell him, smiling too.

We stand, slightly awkward, beads of snow pelting us.

"There's another path?" I ask after a moment, pointing in the direction from which he arrived.

"Not much of a path—but the quickest way. Are we going in our igloo?"

Our. My heart grows.

Once inside, he reaches into his jacket again, and I'm expecting him to extract a new philosophy book, but no. It's a large, slightly floppy, 3D square, which he holds between us on one large palm.

"I've brought this to show you, Nirvana, to help you to imagine..."

It's a relief map of the whole Alps, mountains, passes and valleys. *Brilliant!*

Taking hold of the side nearest me to keep it level, I shuffle a bit closer, catching the piny scent of his shampoo as he points to all the mountains we saw last night, plus Mont Blanc, much further away.

"Here," he indicates a town, Thonon, midway along the croissant of Lac Leman, "is where I go to collège."

"That's a long way," I say.

"Yep, eighteen kilometres each way. There's a school bus."

"I can't imagine that. I can walk to my school. But I hate school as much as skiing."

"Me too," he says.

I'm surprised he doesn't like school. "But what about your philosophy and German? You seem so..." *Into it,*

I want to say, but I don't know how in French. "Interested," I finish weakly.

"I am."

I swivel so I can watch his mouth form the words; how his tongue, teeth and lips—generous lips, I think you'd call them—move to make the different sounds.

"But not in collège or exams or any system of education," he's saying. "I'm searching all these philosophers for how best to *live*."

"For me…" I hesitate, not wanting to sound too wacky again. "For me, we live best when we're connected with nature. Trees are especially important, especially *les*…" I shrug. "Oaks."

"Oaks?"

If only I'd thought to bring my new photo album, I could have shown him Querky.

We look at each other, at a loss. I tug off my glove and with my finger trace the frilly oval outline of an oak leaf on the hard igloo floor.

"*Les chênes*, I think," he says.

"*Chênes*," I echo. "You have these in the Alps?"

"Yeah, though not as many as pines and firs. But why oaks in particular?"

So many reasons flood into my mind. Whenever I was stressed, leaning against our oak's warm, solid trunk soothed me, and being near Querky really comforted Grandad and me when we were first grieving for Nana. But I'm not sure I can explain all that in French, so I go with the practical approach instead.

"Until recently, oaks were much more a part of our everyday lives. They're strong enough to build houses and boats. And when we're with oaks, they give us…

freedom," I decide in the end. "Freedom from the rest of the world."

"Freedom, yes!" Jean-Louis exclaims. "The freedom to live the life we choose. Lots of philosophers have ideas about how to be free, which is why I'm going to study them at university next year."

University. Just hearing the word shuts something down inside of me. I found my future on the *Not Going to Uni* app. Mum was the first of her family to go to uni—to study psychology—and at least there's Claude to guarantee she won't be the last. But I totally get it if that's what means freedom to Jean-Louis.

"Me, I find my freedom *outside* school," I tell him, then chew my lip, unsure what he'll think of this. He's still looking at me, waiting, so I just say it. "I'm a bit of a bad girl." Or so my parents think.

"*Really*, Nirvana?" His mock shock brings out his dimple again. "Tell me about it!"

It's not the easiest thing to explain in French, and we angle ourselves so we're properly facing each other for what turns into a Christmas game of charades that cracks us both up at times. Eventually, though, I get across how I've not only been skipping ski school but bits of *real* school when I could get away with it and why: to build, in my secret woodland workshop, a table for my grandad for when he moves to his new, teeny bungalow. I end with how my parents would go spare if they knew when I'm supposed to be focusing on my GCSEs.

"This...this isn't bad, Nirvana," Jean-Louis says when I've finished. "You're doing what you have to, to be the real you and to make what your grandfather most needs."

My stomach's been pretty much permanently knotted with guilt over my 'stolen' time, but now I smile—in relief, actually—that someone other than me can see the importance of both what I'm trying to do and being true to myself.

"Yep. It'll be a…connection between me as the creator of the table and Grandad as the user. Every day." It's something Ruskin believed in, which I know to be true: when I'm working on the boards, I put love into it, just as some people do with their cooking.

Jean-Louis looks at me, his eyes warm. "You know, you're a philosopher too, Nirvana. And a creator. I have an idea that might perhaps help with your table."

He looks around our igloo as if for inspiration. "How best to describe it…" he ponders. "It's a table in Chalet Ouzon, *une table du berger*—a table for those with little space, like my grandparents who had only a tiny chalet for the summer when they took their cows to the highest pastures."

Berger is a word I know because in French, Rova is a *chien berger*, a sheep dog.

"A shepherd's table," I tell him in English.

Now it's Jean-Louis' turn for charades. As he slowly explains to me, I can tell the table would be ideal: you can fold the tabletop away into a tall, shallow sort of cupboard. A collapsible leg tucks away with it.

I beam at him once he's finished. "I really think I could adapt this for Grandad's new house."

It's a little miner's cottage, near the one where his dad grew up. Dominique can't understand it, calling it backward-looking when he could have a more modern bungalow, but I can see it comforts my grandad, going

41

back to his family's roots when most other parts of his life are changing.

"Thanks so much, Jean-Louis," I tell him. "I'm so..." I throw up my hands, having no idea what 'grateful' is in French.

He looks down, embarrassed.

I check my tracker: time's up. However much I want to spend the rest of the day up here, my family will be on their way back now.

"I have to go," I say, and Jean-Louis scrambles out ahead of me. "You coming too?"

He shakes his head, and again I wonder why he isn't with his family at Christmas.

We stand in the swirling snow, a bit awkward with each other outside our igloo.

"Would you like to keep this, Nirvana?" he asks, holding out the mountain map to me. "To remember the mountains."

My heart squeezes at him offering me this on top of all the listening and help he's already given me today.

"I'd love to, Jean-Louis, but—"

He retracts his arm at my 'but', flushing slightly.

"My parents don't know I came out last night," I hurry on. "I escaped through my bedroom window, so I couldn't explain the map to them."

Now he smiles. "Of course. I should've thought."

"Tomorrow?" I ask instead.

"Tomorrow." There's that dimple again.

Giving a stupid little wave, I set off down the slope.

42

SEVEN

B ACK AT THE chalet, I finally catch up with Sab's reply to
my mountain pic from last night.

> SAB: *Almost as beautiful as my chem textbook!*
> *How's your Christmas?*

Scenes from the day run through my head—stockings
with Claude, the *Ghislaine* episode I fast-forwarded
through, presents with Grandad and Rova on FaceTime...
Our igloo.

> **NIV: Even better than I hoped, thnx.**

> SAB: *Anything to do with the extra French*
> *Speaking and Listening?*

I sink into my pillow. Part of me wishes I'd never
told her about Jean-Louis because how can I explain
our igloo times? This afternoon, even in French, was
the best conversation I've ever had with *anyone*. I can
hardly say that to my best friend! But most of why I'm
loving this Christmas so much more than I imagined *is*
down to Jean-Louis. In one short afternoon, he has made
me feel so much happier about being me. It's hard to
explain to Sab without being hurtful, though, because

the mountains are not the only new world he's spreading before me; there's also Montaigne, the shepherd's table and who knows what else before I have to go home?

> **NIV: It IS just talking.**
>
> *SAB: So you HAVE seen Romeo again.*
>
> **NIV: Romeo was Italian, you noddy!**

We adopted 'noddy' after our chemistry teacher called us a pair of noddies in Year 8 for something in the lab I have to studiously avoid remembering.

> *SAB: I know, Double-Noddy! So tell me his name so I don't have to call him Romeo.*
>
> **NIV: You don't have to call him anything. But he's called Jean-Louis.**

She doesn't reply—another ruse to make me say more. Refusing to play into her hands, I tell her: **Gotta go—out for tea.** Which is true. But also, this…connection with Jean-Louis, it's too new, too special to analyse myself never mind let Sab loose on it.

WE EVENTUALLY MANAGE to prise Claude away from his presents by bringing the snowman I made him to the resto with us. Dominique banned the ukulele, thank God, threatening to say some very nasty things to Uncle Graham about it.

On the way over, the village is pretty busy, for a remote village on a mountain pass. I try to prepare myself for if we bump into Jean-Louis, with or without his family. Would I speak? Would he? And if so, how would I explain it? That we met on the pistes?

But it doesn't happen. At the resto, a kindly woman in her sixties shows us to a round table in the corner; Monsieur Gilbert must be in the kitchen. The whole place looks much jollier after dark, with its fairy lights, candles and, best of all, blazing log-burner.

While the mums drink *kir royal*, flavoured fizzy wine, they and Claude, who is sitting between them, chatter non-stop in French about their time in the *grand secteur*—the advanced ski area at the top of the mountain that I'll never get to.

"What about all those moguls?" Claude says to his *maman*, his eyes gleaming.

Not even caring what one is, I sit back in my chair and observe them. Despite the magic day, I'm suddenly… sad. In just two hours, a crevice has opened between us. This thrilling experience they've shared fills half of it; my secret igloo and Jean-Louis fill the other, along with the answers I've already had to invent:

To Dominique—*How's the skiing going?* Much the same as yesterday. (Not.)

To Claude—*How's Moustache today?* Late. (I do my utmost not to lie to my little brother.)

To Mum—*Are you enjoying 'it' more?* Definitely! (Now I've found a far better 'it' for my afternoons!)

I don't get a kick out of hiding stuff. I only do it when I have to, having found honesty often *isn't* the best policy with adults. Right now, though, I'd love to talk about *my* afternoon. I toy with a scenario in my head where I lean into a gap in their conversation, I say:

"I spent the afternoon sitting in an igloo with a French lad, looking at a map of all the mountains and talking about the hours I've spent working on Querky. And he suggested the best sort of table to make for Grandad."

Dominique's eyebrows'd never come down again!

Then the interrogation would start—*When? How? Where?*

Secrets and lies, they breed a family of knots. I can't ever tell them about Jean-Louis without mentioning the igloo, or the igloo without revealing I'm missing ski school. Likewise, I can't mention Grandad's table without admitting to my hidden place and my 'stolen' time there—at least until it's made.

It would only end in bans: no more Jean-Louis; no Grove; no Niv-plan.

So, of course, I sit back, keep quiet and watch my family. Sitting around our table, we're like that big wheel of Reblochon cheese we bought at the *fromagerie* on our way from Geneva airport. If you took out a Nirvana-shaped quarter, the three of them would still be a whole cheese. They'd ooze together, fill the space I'd left. That's going to happen anyway over the next two years and beyond. Ten years, a whole decade, the mums will have with Claude but not me.

The gap's only going to get wider.

So what happens to the quarter that's me?

I look at Mum. We had *nine* years of us two, Rova and my grandparents. Now we're a new family. Her cheeks glow and she's wearing her wavy hair down tonight. I can't remember her ever looking happier.

Grandad and Rova, they're not going to be around forever. I've got to look to my future. Wherever that takes me.

Maybe it'll really lead through the door to my donor dad. Maybe I wouldn't have to keep so many secrets from him. Maybe, like Jean-Louis seems to, he'd appreciate some of the real-Niv bits Mum struggles with.

The appearance of the much-talked-of *raclette* machine soon jolts me back to the here and now, bringing us all back together. It's a round, metal plate with a gas burner underneath, which the waitress lights. We then cook our own choice of peppers, mushrooms, ham and potatoes on the segment in front of us. Along with a salad, the waitress brings us freshly melted *raclette* cheese again and again till we can eat no more. It's delicious and fun, even though it's not our traditional one.

Once the bill's all paid, we're making our way to the door when Monsieur Gilbert appears from the kitchen. Claude and I burst out laughing.

"Good evening, young man," he says, smiling through the fake handlebar moustache—he must've worn it all day!—as he hands Claude a bag of brightly wrapped *bonbons.* The mums are mystified by all this.

"In exchange for this wonderful moustache," he explains to them.

Outside, I hook Claude in to me to nub the top of his head, dead proud of the unlikely connection he sparked this morning between himself and the resto owner I reckon needed a bit of cheering up.

"Gerroff!" he squeals as he opens his bag of sweets.

Knowing he loves it really, I nick one off him.

We trudge back to the chalet, stuffed with our Alpine Christmas dinner, and I gaze up at the balconies of each lit apartment, wondering which could be Jean-Louis', whether he might even appear. Would we wave?

THERE'S STILL NO sign of him, and having only had a few hours' sleep last night, I'm in bed early. Usually, I insist on staying up till midnight on Christmas Day to make it last as long as possible, but this year, I'm not sad the day is ending. There's too much to look forward to tomorrow.

EIGHT

I WAKE UP RESTED and still happy—no massive anticlimax this Boxing Day: every igloo meeting is at least as good as Christmas Day!

No one revises on Boxing Day, do they? But sitting at the little pine desk in my room, where I dumped my revision books the day we arrived, I make some sketches of what Jean-Louis described yesterday—what I'm now thinking of as a miner's table, a variation on Jean-Louis' shepherd's version.

All the time I'm drawing, planning in my head, Jean-Louis feels close; this is all inspired by *him*. It makes it even more of a pleasure.

So far, since Alz brought the planks to the Grove in September, I've planed and sanded all twenty of them, which takes some time when all I've got is hand tools and snippets of stolen time here and there. Now I know exactly what I want to build, I mark measurements on my design. Finding an indoor workspace to move into was to have been my main mission over the Christmas holidays, till Dominique sprang this holiday on us. Sab's such a pal, promising to keep an eye out for me: if I'm to cut the boards to size and lay them out, a boggy forest floor is so not the place. 'Course, inside's better for her too in

49

the winter, as she often hangs out with me, avoiding her parents' constant nattering to get on with school work or stuff for their company.

AFTER LUNCH, I'M the first into my ski gear. While Dominique's trying to shoehorn Claude into his salopettes, I peer out of the living room window and up towards our igloo, invisible in the mist and snow.

"Raring to get out there, Niv?" Mum asks, making me jump.

You bet! Just not in the way you mean.

I turn to face her, over a splash of Claude's toys in the middle of the room.

"Skiing's not for me, Mum," I tell her. "For me, it's pointless without something to see."

I toe the rubble of wooden pieces of the snowman on the pine floor, abandoned by Claude in preference for brighter, louder stuff like dressing-up gear and musical instruments.

I've put off telling her for so long, but now it can't wait any longer. At least this is a something she *can't* stop. But I'd sooo rather do it *with* her approval.

Now or never. The first person *ever* to hear my life plan.

I look Mum in the eye.

"We can't help what we are and aren't drawn to, Mum." I take a big breath. "That's why it's such good news that I've found the perfect solution for me, after Year Eleven."

I can practically see the tension in her shoulders and face, her hair now scraped back for skiing, as she braces herself for a Niv bombshell.

"It's for an apprenticeship."

50

Her forehead creases. She and Dominique are really academic—both went to uni. But as my Nana used to say, *the apple can fall far from the tree.*

"In what?" she asks.

"Joinery," I tell her, nodding in my effort to convince her. "It's the perfect blend of being practical *and* creative."

Mum's face has shut down as suddenly and completely as a computer screen.

"I'm aiming high, Mum. I would get paid by any firm who takes me on, and I'd also get the equivalent of two A' levels at college. At the end of it, I'll be able to make all kinds of furniture. Windows, doors—stairs even."

I throw my hands out in a sort of *voilà, there you have it* gesture.

"Is this cold feet about your mocks, Niv? Even though you've had a bit of a break over Christmas, you've had your head down this term. They'll be fine."

A pang twangs my stomach for all the times I wasn't at Sab's doing homework or revision, occasionally not even at school, but at the Grove.

"I know Dominique's a bit too...heavy-handed sometimes," Mum's saying, "buying you an eReader, making revision timetables...but she only wants what's best for you."

"That's just it, Mum. What's best for me isn't what you and Dominique think it is. At all."

She opens her mouth, then can't seem to find the words—as if it's never even crossed her mind we might think differently about things!

"It's my hands I'm good with, and that's what I love too." I'm speaking fast before she can find her words again. "I hate it at Presdale Girls'. I hate sitting at a desk all day long, every day the same. I want to be out there, making."

"This is a...a...cop-out," Mum says. "You're worried you're not going to do well, so you're setting your sights lower."

My blood starts to fizz.

"Lower? Lower?" My voice has gone higher! "I've told you, Mum, a Level 4 NVQ is the same as two A' levels. It even gives you UCAS points."

Not that I'll ever need them.

"NVQ," she chunters as if it's a swear word. "You could take French for A' level, maybe a new subject. Even Art."

Even Art! The fizzing becomes buzzing.

"You're such an education snob!" I tell her.

"A' levels—*any* A' levels. Keep your options open," she sweeps on. "You can always do an apprenticeship at eighteen. But you can't change direction once you've gone down such a vocational route, can you?"

I blow out a breath, trying to cool myself down.

"Woodworking *is* my vocation, Mum. I won't want to change. Ever."

"But you've not been to Hackspace for months now, anyway."

I snort. "Only cos I wasn't allowed!"

Given her utter rejection of anything joinery-related, it's now horribly clear there's no way I can tell Mum about the table. Not till it's done.

"How can we know this isn't just a phase, Niv? And if not, take it up again as a hobby once your exams are over, eh, love?"

52

"My woodwork's *not* a phase or a hobby!" I'm boiling inside now, and it's ramping up my volume again. "The application form's already filled in on my laptop at home. And apprenticeships don't even need parental permission anymore." Which is true, though I'd way prefer to do it with her blessing.

She stalks past me, to the window, accidentally kicking some of Claude's toys. I turn to look at her gazing out at the fuzzy white.

Who's the teenager here?!

Deliberately, I drop my shoulders and reset my volume.

"I've still got my covering letter to draft this week. And I'd *love* you to look at it when I'm done, Mum. Cos I need to send it before the end of the year."

A sharp shake of her head.

"I can't win!" I tell her. "You and Dominique have gone on and on at me for months about deciding my next stage. Now I have, you don't like it." I move to stand at the window next to her. "Why waste two years when an apprenticeship's exactly what I want?"

"Because, Niv…" Now she turns to me. "You can do so much better!"

WHAT? My hand actually goes to my mouth. Of all the things she could say, this is the worst. For a moment, I'm literally gobsmacked.

"No, I friggin' well couldn't!" I say. "Nothing, *NOTHING* is better than turning something that was a tree into something people need. So, when the right firm offers me an apprenticeship, I'll be taking it. Wherever in the UK it is!"

Eyebrows high, Mum casts one of her *are you quite finished?* looks my way.

Shaking my head, I grab my coat and backpack from by the door and stomp out of the chalet, down to the drying room to force my feet into my ski boots. As I walk down the drive, I pass the four-person snow family Claude and I built the day we arrived—now a white rectangle. I give it a good kick with my boot.

NINE

NOT WAITING FOR the rest of them, I grab my skis—for show—and carry on stomping in the ridiculously relentless snow all the way down to the piste, where I stop for a couple of minutes till the three of them have vanished. Then I stomp all the way up to Jean-Louis, my head swarming with *you can do so much better... settling... easier...*

So easy, is it, Mum? Getting half a tree to the Grove in secret, stealing back snippets of my own time to make the table Grandad needs? All the designing, measuring, physical prep. *Easy*?! What do you think it's like having half your genetic make-up being all but a mystery? Might look easy when you're close to both your parents and can see all of yourself reflected in your bio family, like you and Dominique can.

This is the bit I didn't want to complicate my argument with now: that my creativity must be from my donor dad. That's *why* it's so alien to Mum and wasted on her.

She and Dominique have told Claude and me how kind and helpful our donors were, but that's where it ends. They've only ever called them donors, discouraging us from using 'donor dad' or father because a parent is someone who's around, who *nurtures* you.

But it's not that simple. When you have instincts and interests you can't see anywhere else in your family, it leaves you feeling…like a misfit.

I reach the top of the steep path without even noticing! As I round the corner, I can make out Jean-Louis' shape already outside our igloo, thank heavens.

"You okay, Nirvana?" he asks, his tone slightly anxious as he peers at me through the fat, falling flakes.

"No." My voice quavers now somebody's bothered about my feelings.

He steps even closer, reaches his hand towards me, hesitates, retracts it.

"What happened?" he asks.

My shoulders slump. "An argument with my mother."

His mouth gives a sympathetic shrug. "*Ç'est normal!*"

His hand reaches out again, and gentle fingers sweep the snow off my hair.

For some reason, I feel a whole lot lighter.

"WANT TO TALK about it?" he asks once we're inside.

I huff out a big breath and search for the right French words. "I finally told her I want to leave school in September to do…an apprenticeship?"

He nods. "*Une apprentissage.*"

"In woodwork," I explain. "To build furniture."

"Sounds perfect for you."

I look at him and nod. *Of course it is! If he can see it, when he's only known me two days, why can't my own mother?*

"And yet she was angry and, worse, disappointed that I'm not like her, as if that's the best way for *me* to be. She went to university and doesn't value me being good with my hands."

"*Zut*, that's difficult! It's the opposite with me. My mother won't support me going to university. She insists I've got to earn my own living next year when I leave college."

"Maybe we should swap mothers," I joke.

He gives me a pained look. "You wouldn't want that, Nirvana. Mine mocks my interest in philosophy—'How can thinking earn you a living?'"

I chew the side of my lip. I've felt horribly put down by Mum today, but now I've calmed down a bit, I don't think she meant to and she'd certainly never mock me.

"You could teach philosophy," I suggest, trying to answer his mother for him. I know from Dominique that all French teenagers have to learn some philosophy. "Better still, write essays, like Montaigne."

His mouth gives a sad shrug. "Who would read them? Montaigne was an aristocrat. He didn't need to make a penny. Teaching, I don't fancy that."

"Your father?" I ask. "What does he think?"

Now his mouth relaxes.

"Papa finds the differences between him and me intriguing. He gets why philosophy's important to me and supports me in whatever I want to do."

"Ah, there you're lucky!"

I tell Jean-Louis how it reassures me to think my practical part could come from my donor; that one parent at least might support my woodwork career.

Then we're quiet for a moment while he draws crisscrosses on the igloo floor with his finger before he looks up at me again.

"I suppose we may never know where all the parts of us come from. And happily, we're not always like our parents. At all."

"Your mum?" I check.

He gives a sharp nod.

"My mum makes me feel I'm such a disappointment—need to try harder." I shrug. "Maybe I wouldn't feel like such an outsider if I gave up the apprenticeship idea."

"No, don't give up, Nirvana!" His tone's urgent. "Otherwise, you'd be a stranger to *yourself*, and that's far, far worse."

I sway back a little at the force of his conviction.

"I think," he says, his cheek dimpling as he looks at me sideways from under his eyelashes, "maybe you have a little of *druide* in you, Nirvana, no?"

I open my mouth and close it again. Mum's often teased Grandad and me about being a pair of tree-hugging pagans in the way we like to mark the seasons, but never druids!

"I've been reading up on oaks," he goes on, "and I see that 'druid' essentially means someone with a love and knowledge of oaks and their importance to people."

I smile and shrug. "Then yes, I am!"

Warming to the idea of being a druid, I sit up a bit taller.

"I believe we each have an essential part of us," he goes on, "natural and innate. The *âme*."

58

I shrug. I've never heard that before. "Maybe the soul or the spirit?"

"*Esprit*? No. Maybe more the *soi*."

That, I have heard. "Yes! The self."

He nods. "Our *âme* must be expressed. Otherwise..." He spreads his arms wide, suggesting *we've lost everything*.

"Yes!" bursts out of me. "That's all I want. To be free to be my 'self'."

Which seems to lead to just the right moment. I unzip my backpack and pull out the memory album Grandad put together for me. I hug it to me for a moment.

"This is the life of our very special oak tree. We even had a name for him."

He smiles when I explain the name, and I shuffle closer to show him the pages of Querky's and our life.

I slow down, I have to, when I come to the final page: Querky in his summer prime. What's next is the most important thing I need to get across to Jean-Louis.

"That's the last photo in this book," I tell him. "But there's one more, one I have to keep from my grandad."

Having packed my album away, I scroll through my gallery and hold the image out in front of Jean-Louis: our beautiful, veteran oak's massive trunk and lush canopy, dismembered across the lawn.

"No!" he says, blinking as he looks from my phone to me.

I nod, solemn. "We tried, Grandad and me, to save him. I even slept under him for a whole week!"

As best I can, I explain how friggin' Lancashire Council thought an ugly, new road was more important than an ancient, *noble* tree. A healthy, *living* being, with a past and future all of its own. Part of our family.

"This was when I discovered," I tell Jean-Louis, "adults often make the very worst decisions of all."

"Absolutely," he says solemnly.

We're quiet for a moment. Then I smile and ask him, "You haven't guessed?"

I see the realisation dawn, his face lighting up.

"*Ba oui*! You mean, you're building your grandad's table from his own oak tree?"

I nod and fill him in on the whole ironic chain, something only Sab knows otherwise. How, having promised Querky we would use all of him well, Grandad donated his trunk to Hackspace, where it was sliced like a tall loaf. How I went every week for fifteen months, learning my craft, but then, because of exams, my parents banned Hackspace Saturdays. So, my best friend, Sabihah, pressganged her brother into transporting—in the family van—twenty of the oak planks from Manchester to the Grove, the woods near where I live. And the biggest irony—how the loss of our oak led me to knowing how I want to spend my working life—to my apprenticeship.

"Best of all," I conclude, "Grandad's table will also be the project for my apprenticeship application."

He shakes his head, smiling, and draws a circle in the air with his hands. "It's all linked! And resurrecting your tree for both you and your grandfather makes for a happier ending, doesn't it?"

"The best I can do," I tell him. "At least our oak wasn't lost for nothing."

"Now it's even more important I help with your project," he says.

"You could tell me if this looks anything like a shepherd's table." I pull my sketch pad out of my backpack and show him.

"Yes, it's something like this," he says. "But would it help to see the real thing?"

Wide-eyed, I nod vigorously.

"Well, then, we could go to Chalet Ouzon?"

"Yes!" I say at once, in English, grinning as widely as him. "Let's do it!"

An adventure! More time together!

"I just need to work out how," he says, bringing us back down to earth again. "It's an hour's walk each way. So, if we only have two hours..."

I grit my teeth. Friggin' timetables, friggin' controlling parents! Do I just come clean with them? Tell them I've given up skiing and found myself a French...friend instead? Objections—Mum's then Dominique's—throng my brain, along with the very real terror they'll escort me to my ski lessons and I'll never see Jean-Louis again.

"Leave it with me, Nirvana," he says.

I nod. "Where there's a will there's a way, my wise grandmother used to say."

Once we've managed to translate that between us, all too soon, it's time for *à demains* again.

TEN

BACK AT THE chalet, it's as if Mum and I had never had the argument. This is her usual tactic—sweep the uncomfortable stuff under the carpet and hope it stays there. Not that I want to keep talking about it either if she's going to carry on closing her mind to my apprenticeship. I'm more certain than ever now: talking to Jean-Louis about it has cemented my decision, reminded me of the rightness of our oak leading to my future. And Mum's reaction, as the first ever person to hear my apprenticeship ambition, still smarts.

She's reading one of Claude's new books to him anyway—*Billy and the Minpins,* a real hit with him—so I go to the kitchen and chop vegetables for Dominique, who's making *bœuf bourguignon.* She loves cooking on school holidays and weekends. Talking about the recipe seems the safest topic, and it actually reminds me of all the times we used to cook happily together when I was a little girl before Claude, before I started to grow up, I suppose, and diverged from the version of me she and Mum would prefer.

"Your French is improving nicely, Nirvan-ah," Dominique tells me after a while.

I look at her in astonishment. I hadn't even realised I'd been speaking it, but it seems totally natural now to speak

French to a French person, even Dominique, whom I've spent years refusing to talk French with!

"You see, as I said, the ski lessons are also French lessons."

No! I want to say as I slice through a carrot, *it's all down to Jean-Louis!* But now I find, instead of my stomach rolling with guilt at my secrets, I remember Jean-Louis saying I'm not *méchante* at all, just doing what I have to. If only I could introduce Jean-Louis to Dominique, I know she'd really like him. Claude would be asking him what it's like to live in a ski station, and Mum'd be fascinated by his interest in philosophy.

"Did you see the poster for tomorrow's workshop in the community room under the resto?" Dominique is asking. "We are going to take Claude. It is for making *baguettes magiques.*"

She laughs at my expression. "No, nothing to do with bread sticks. It means magic wand! They will be making them out of wood."

"Let me take him," I say. "I'd enjoy it anyway. You and Mum could go out skiing for the morning."

"Really? *Merci!* That would be so kind, *chou-chou.*"

I smile. She used to call me that when I was little. She kisses the top of my head as she passes by to the cooker.

MUM AND DOMINIQUE decide to watch a French film as soon as Claude's in bed. I go to my room instead. As I go to close my shutters, I've a faint hope the snow might have cleared as it did on Christmas Eve. But it's wild beyond the balcony, the wind whipping frozen beads in all directions. No way will Jean-Louis be out there tonight. But another night? A clear night, like Christmas Eve? We could go to his grandparents' chalet at night, couldn't we? I bounce onto my bed, dying to suggest it to him. If only we'd swapped phone numbers…

I look at my phone and know I owe Sab a message. But I talked out Mum's and my argument with Jean-Louis. What *could* I tell her of our igloo time today? Jean-Louis finally opening up about his parents? Him supporting me with the apprenticeship she doesn't yet know about? I'm gonna have to find the right time to fill her in on that.

The pile of books on my desk catches my eye, all of them untouched.

NIV: Aggh! Only 8 days till mocks!

A pain shoots across my chest. That means, including tonight, only five nights till we go home.

NIV: How's it going?

SAB: Bleurgh. Done anything but French yet?

NIV: Just going to finish E of Eden.

SAB: You can tell me the ending then.

Sab needs a film of it if she's to get to the end of the story. I know she'll be reading all sorts into my not mentioning 'Romeo'. But I'll be home all too soon, and there'll be no wrong conclusions to reach then.

I put down my phone, pick up my eReader and lean back against the pine headboard. I do actually want to know how it goes for Cal when he meets the mother who left him at birth. Once I've turned out my bedside lamp, I read by the backlight of my eReader, and I can't stop, right till the end of the book.

I sigh as I slide my device onto the bedside table. I should have known from the title this was never going to be a happy read. Cal's dad was hell-bent on keeping his mum from him for the best of reasons: she turned out to be a psychopath who wanted to abort him!

I'm quite sure my donor dad's no such monster, though! And maybe my irresistible pull towards creating and carpentry *does* come from him. But even if it didn't, I bet *he'll* appreciate that part of me if I decide to contact him when I'm eighteen.

In the deep dark, I think back over growing up at Oak Vista. Knowing she was gay and not having met anyone, Mum decided to have me quite young to enlist her parents' help while they were still able. With Mum, my grandparents, Rova and that amazing garden and Querky, my childhood *was* Eden, and it'll hurt to shift too far east of it when it's looking increasingly like Mum *won't* be supporting my woodwork career.

I'm not afraid to go for what I want. Earlier with Dominique, I got a glimpse of how approval feels, over my French and taking Claude to the workshop tomorrow: a lovely warm glow. But if I give up on my apprenticeship, that wouldn't be Eden either. As Jean-Louis said, I'd be a stranger to myself.

How can I win when either way I lose so much?

ELEVEN

THIS BRILLIANT COUPLE'S running the *baguette magique* workshop. They've brought branches of different kinds of wood to choose from. Rashly, the man offers to take on Claude, leaving me to work on a wand of my own. While I gently whittle down this most beautiful piece of hazel, I can't shut out the fact that Mum won't want to encourage me by showing any interest in it later. That hurts because we used to be so close.

Was Jean-Louis ever close to his mum? I wonder. Maybe all teenagers go through this, and I'm not enjoying it one bit.

With the repetitive action of my whittling soothing me, I try to put myself in Mum's shoes again. Am I *really* that big of a problem? How would I feel if one of my kids wanted to take a route I didn't approve of? I would have to adjust a bit; I can see that. But I wouldn't try to force her into something she really didn't want to do—would always struggle to do. Surely, you'd rather your child was happy than squash her into the version of herself you wanted for her?

I hold my hazel stick out in front of me. Already ingrained with knots and whorls, it doesn't need any adornment; just shaping and sealing with a clear veneer,

which allows its nutty colour, its true nature—its *soi*—
to show through.

AFTER LUNCH, DOMINIQUE randomly decides to take an
interest in my progress on the pistes so I actually have to
clamp on my skis today.

"Look, Nirvan-ah," she says, from the edge of the
piste, "it is your instructor, *n'est- çe-pas?*"

My stomach nosedives all but down to my feet.
Not only is Moustache early for the first time ever, but
hearing Dominique, he turns and opens his arms to let
me go before him at the end of a short crocodile headed
towards the bottom of the blue piste, to where a yellow
triangle warns *Téléski difficile!*

"Go on, *chou!*" Dominique calls.

Well and truly trapped, I have no choice but to slip-
slide my skis after the others. On the plus side, when
I reach the top, I'll be just around the corner from
our igloo, and really, it's just another lift pull, isn't it?
You keep your weight in your heels and enjoy the ride.

When I actually see what I'm up against, my pulse
rockets. The narrow rut you get pulled up must be
a hundred times steeper than the one on the green piste.
I'm honestly starting to feel sick. I'm through the barrier
now though, where you have to swipe your lift pass.
The point of no return.

I try to breathe. Only three in front of me. I watch
carefully. *It is just the same,* I tell myself. *Just steeper:
Get your skis pointing in the same direction, facing the same
way the drag lift's going*—always a good idea.

"*Ç'est toi*," Moustache says, giving me a little push in the back.

"I can't...I'm not sure..."

"Then I show you," he says, somehow managing to manoeuvre his bulky squareness past me.

It all happens so quickly, it's no help whatsoever. About a metre up the slope, he disappears into a cloud of snow, leaving me all on my own.

I swallow and look behind me. I *could* take my skis off, duck under the barrier and disappear back to the ski racks.

But the door of the little hut has opened, and the drag-lift operator appears next to me. I feel my eyes widen. It's her! Ghislaine the smoker, with a miserable look on her face. What's she got to be so grumpy about anyway? It's not exactly stressful, sitting in a cosy shed most of the day, listening to music!

"*Viens!*" she snaps, as if there were a whole queue of eager skiers beyond me instead of white space.

Yeah, well, what is beyond you, I tell her in my head, is being nice to people—customers, actually—you friggin' misery!

She thrusts a pole into my hands, and it sets off uphill, yanking me into the air then after it before I can even get my skis lined up.

Yiiiiiiiikes!

The button that should be under my bum is in front of me as the pole drags me at full stretch up the mountain. I last maybe four metres before it feels like my arms are about to be wrenched from my body and I have to let go.

I'm not a cartoon character, though, and don't end up flat on my stomach like I'd imagined. Just in a painful, contorted mass of my soft limbs and the hard, heavy metal of my skis.

Arggh! The empty button behind me clips the back of my head, and I launch my top half to the side before the next one knocks me out.

My legs are still skewed in opposite directions, and even if I get them un-skewed enough to stand up, I can't ski down this mini mountain. I squirm around to look down at Ghislaine. *Do something! Press the frigging red button!*

Instead, she's standing there, a spectre in the snow but still clear enough for me to see the huge smirk on her face.

Revenge?

I'm on my own, I realise.

Wincing, I manage to shift my weight up enough to bring both legs to the same side and try to prise myself off the ground, but it's impossible with skis on. I reach around to press down on the back of the bindings with the heel of one hand, but I can't get enough weight on it from this angle. I turn back the way most of my body is facing and take a moment. Angry tears are pricking, which never happens.

Next thing I know, my skis are being lifted from my boots, and a strong hand is under my arm, pulling me firmly to my feet. Jean-Louis!

No idea how you knew, nor do I really care, I think as he scoops up the skis I never want to see again. Carrying all my clobber over one shoulder—he's surprisingly strong for someone who seems to spend most of his time philosophising—he walks on the lower side of me so I don't slip and steers me by my left arm across the piste to the other side, to what must be the route he takes.

Jean-Louis stands in front of me, shielding me from the driving snow.

"You want to try again, Nirvana?" he asks.

"No way!" I tell him. "Long story, but I was only trying to get to our igloo."

He smiles wide, and I reflect it back at him. I've done a lot of smiling these last few days.

"Great! So, I'll take your skis down to the rack, then see you up there."

I open my mouth—I should take my own gear down, yet it's easier for him in walking boots—then close it again and nod. I'll wait here for him.

After he's dropped my skis off, he doesn't head straight back up the track but strides to the little cabin, which, it turns out, has doors on each side.

He thumps on the door.

Ghislaine flings it open.

I can't make out words from up here, but the tone is clear. His arms fly about in a wide span. She stands, her arms folded against him.

Go, Jean-Louis! He's doing this for me. My heart swells.

As he turns away, she disappears back into her pit, and I hurry up the hill as best I can. He didn't intend for me to see him tearing a strip off her.

INSIDE OUR IGLOO, I at once feel safe, hidden from Moustache, Ghislaine, my mothers, cocooned from the

70

clanking of metal and the shouts of skiers who actually enjoy it.

Jean-Louis' head and shoulders appear. I shift sideways to give him room.

In the dimness, I feel more than see the anger still coiled up in him. Surely this can't all be for me? He's leaning forward on his knees which are drawn up into his body, his arms wrapped around them. Brooding. I miss the usual optimistic Jean-Louis.

"Thank you," I say. "For helping me."

He does a scoffing sort of sigh. "*She* should have helped you."

I shrug. "We had a bit of an...encounter in the resto on Christmas morning. My little brother and I told her she shouldn't be smoking inside."

Getting her own back. I've no idea how to say that in French, and I've certainly never seen adults play this tit-for-tat game.

Jean-Louis gazes at me in disgust, shaking his head. "I didn't know about this."

My forehead knits. Why would he?

"What *is* her problem?" I ask. "Has she suffered some terrible tragedy or something that's made her so...bitter?"

He shakes his head, his mouth taut. "She's a monster," he declares.

I flinch at the word and this tone I've not heard from him before, and he seems so sure.

"It's not news to me, adults being so very wrong," I tell him. "But she seems far worse than a child— a *cruel* child."

"And you could've been hurt," he says.

It's true. I'm not sure what would have happened if he'd not come to my rescue. But I can't work out whether he ripped into her solely for my sake or his as well. Somehow this doesn't feel like a first. Maybe it's village politics.

"Is she your neighbour?"

He snorts. "Everyone's your neighbour in this village."

I shudder at the thought of seeing that cow every day, or living in such a claustrophobic place that you get to this point with each other.

We fall silent. I'm searching for a way to change the subject, distract him.

"Do you have any brothers or sisters?" I ask him, in a faint link to Claude.

"Just me," he says, more miserable than ever.

An only child. It suddenly hits me. For all the age gap and personality differences between Claude and me, for all we're not even related by blood, I'm really grateful that someone else shares our parents, our situation.

I glance at Jean-Louis' rigid body language and tight lips. Right!

"I took my brother to the *atelier de bois* under the resto this morning," I say, reaching inside my ski jacket. "And I made this."

He takes it from me, running his fingers down it and looking at it carefully.

"The wood is hazel," I tell him. "I don't know in French."

"*Noisetier*," he tells him. "It's beautiful."

"I'd like you to have it, Jean-Louis. A late Christmas present."

72

Our eyes meet, and I blush. Maybe he'll think it's silly, childish, that I'm trying to banish his mood with a magic wand! But I know now, I was making it for him all along.

"Thank you, Nirvana," he says quietly.

"No, thanks to you," I say, trying to cover my embarrassment, "for rescuing me today."

We fall silent again for quite a while.

"You must miss being with your friends from home," he says eventually, still holding the *baguette magique*.

Where's this coming from? I daren't even hope he's fishing to find out if I have a boyfriend.

"I miss my closest friend most of all," I tell him.

He tips his head.

"My sheep dog. She's the same age as me now." Mum adopted her while she was pregnant, and we grew up together.

"Ahh, I love dogs!" Jean-Louis exclaims. "But my mother's never allowed me to have one."

"Because you live in an apartment?" Every time I'm in the village, I wonder where he lives.

He shrugs. "Partly."

I look at him, wondering why else. He doesn't seem inclined to talk about the other reasons.

I tell him about Sabihah, how we bonded over not being the highest achievers in our ultra-competitive girls' school; why she comes to the Grove with me whenever she can; how it's a place to breathe, away from parental pressure about school and the family business; and how, while I'm away, she's looking for an indoor workspace for me *and* her.

73

He recovers his smiliness as he listens, seeming... relieved somehow.

"Sab's still waiting for photos of the Alps by day," I tell him, "but..." I shrug. "Does it never stop snowing in the day?"

"It stops when it wants to stop."

I smile at his accepting way of thinking about the weather.

"I'll do my best to find you a view before you leave, Nirvana," he says.

I blink and smile again, touched more by his desire to help than the likelihood of him being successful.

"What about you?" I ask. "Are your friends more from *collège* or in the village?"

"Because of living so remotely, the friend I see most lives in Le Biot, the village at the foot of the mountain. Marc," he adds.

No mention of a girlfriend, and I've not sensed at any point that he's gay.

I nod then check my tracker. "Must go—or the game is up," I finish off in English.

"Zhe game is oop?" he asks in the cutest accent.

"I don't know where the idiom's from, but basically, if my parents discover I'm not skiing, I'll never be free to come again."

"Which is why we have our igloo," he tells me. "So they don't."

Smiling, I let my eyes roam around the dome of our lovely, secret igloo.

A refuge for rebels.

An escape from parents.

As I'm slip-sliding my way back down the track, I stop suddenly and slap my hand to my forehead: I'm an idiot! Why didn't I tell him my idea about going at night to Chalet Ouzon or swap phone numbers? Time is running out! Only four nights to go—a countdown that has started to regularly butt into my brain.

Tomorrow, we *must* arrange something. If he's still up for it.

BACK AT THE chalet, from the safety of my lovely big bed, I tell Sab:

> **NIV: Humiliating drag-lift tumble today... almost brained.**

She's typing already.

> SAB: *Safer in an igloo with Romeo. Jean-Louis, I mean!*

I roll my eyes.

> **NIV: It was all down to this Ghoulish Ghislaine I keep seeing all over the village. She abandoned me and my skull to a series of metal clubs!**

> SAB: *It's a wonder you're still conscious!*

I sniff and hesitate.

NIV: Jean-Louis happened to be passing and helped me off the piste.

I brace myself.

SAB: Of course he 'happened to be passing'.

I have to laugh. While it's made a good story afterwards, I can't forget Jean-Louis' tense, unhappy body language in our igloo, and it pains me inside to think of going home, leaving him on his own with *her* on the loose.

But what can I do?

TWELVE

I GET ON WITH it straight after breakfast, the covering letter for any apprenticeship matches that come my way in the new year. If Mum's gone quiet about it because she thinks she's won, she couldn't be more wrong. I gave her a chance to get involved, and she threw it back in my face.

It doesn't feel like work at all as I describe the miner's table I'm going to submit as my portfolio. I'm going to have to suggest to Jean-Louis my idea for going to his grandparents' chalet on one of the three nights I have left. It'd make a huge difference to see how the table hinges onto the upright and to measure all the components.

Three nights before I go home. I shunt the painful fact right back out of my head.

When 'ski time' comes—not that I'll *ever* be putting my feet near those metal torments again—Dominique's fleeting interest in my progress has been eclipsed by Claude having graduated ski school altogether. The three of them will now be together on the higher *secteur* every afternoon. *Tant mieux*, as Jean-Louis would say— so much the better that we have an hour longer.

I slow down as I reach the last bend, not wanting to arrive at our igloo all out of breath.

Jean-Louis' outline takes shape through the whiteout, firming up the nearer I get till I can see a grim expression on his face. My heart pauses. What?

Then I see.

"BUT WHERE...BUT WHAT...?" I stutter, stupid, stupefied.

His arms are wrapped around himself, gazing into the snow, out beyond the *col*.

Our igloo's flattened. Annihilated. Like it never existed. And the machine would have had to go waaay out of its way to smash it like this.

"So..." I try again. "The piste basher. But why? Why now? A new driver maybe?"

Still he gazes as if he can't hear me. He's in shock.

I step nearer, stand right next to him, so close our sleeves are touching.

"What a pity," I say gently.

A real pity.

If I'd been the first here, I'd have been upset too, but not as devastated as him. If only my wand really was magic.

"We can build another," I tell him, my voice all cheery.

Even as I say it, I know it wouldn't be the same. Our first igloo is where we met, *how* we met. A shared shelter before we even knew each other. But still...

"She'd only destroy it again."

His tone is flat, defeated, as he speaks out into the snow.

"Who? Who would?"

"Her!" He flings out an arm towards the cabin at the bottom of the piste.

Oh, Ghislaine!

"Really? You think she told them to do it? Knock down the igloo?"

"I *know* she did. Normally, the drivers are so careful not to destroy even a snowman."

Just for calling her out on not doing her job? The bitch!

He heaves the heaviest sigh I've ever heard. It's a serious feud he's got going on with this woman. I could tell right from that first time in the car park, she's what Grandad would call 'a nasty piece of work'.

We need to talk, Jean-Louis and me. Proper igloo time. But our refuge is gone. We have nowhere else to go—not his, wherever that is, not mine. And we're getting cold, fast.

"Let's walk," I suggest. "At least it's more sheltered in the woods."

I find us a narrow, un-trodden route through the thick of friendly, silent trees next to the site of our... former igloo.

When the way widens out, I wait for him to come alongside me, and we stumble over the hidden bumps of tree roots. What's bothering him most? The person who destroyed our igloo or that we don't have it anymore? I want the upbeat Jean-Louis back; his sadness to vanish. But the right words won't come, and even if they did, I'm not sure words can make things right for him.

So I just breathe, take in the sweetest air. It's a gorgeous little wood. I can count on one hand the number of times I've seen the Grove in snow, and even then, the birches had shed their leaves, of course. Here, the snowy evergreens make their presence felt by sharing their stillness and calm.

Tree therapy.

I hoped Jean-Louis would feel their solidarity with us, but now we've reached the sharp end, the V of the wedge, and he's still radiating tension.

"This wood has two different types of conifers?" I check with him, gazing at the trees surrounding us.

"*Ba oui*. The pines and the spruces. You can tell the difference by their needles."

He reaches out for the nearest branch and shakes off the snow.

"You see how these needles are growing singly? And you can roll one easily between your fingers."

I wriggle off my gloves, and it's true. The needles feel to have four sides, which help them rotate.

"So, it's a spruce," he tells me.

"So, this one's a pine?" I say, turning to a different tree with its needles in pairs.

He runs his bare palm along the sprouting bristles, releasing its clean, perfumed scent.

"I used to make pine syrup from trees like this with my grandparents."

"Good?"

He smiles at last. "Delicious, if you add some sugar. Like maple syrup, I suppose."

I smile back, happy *he's* happier. But now it's time to turn back, to ground zero.

"I don't like leaving you here on your own," I tell him, trying one last time to get him to come back down to the village with me.

He shakes his head, back to fretting now we're confronted again by the destruction of our igloo.

I can't stay any longer, I can't. But I also won't let this be the end of what should have been one of our very few igloo times. I plant myself in front of him.

"You know this village so well. If you find the right place, she'll never know about it. No one will. Tomorrow afternoon, let's build the most secret, most beautiful igloo. And let's build it together this time, Jean-Lou."

I don't even know where it came from, but at 'Jean-Lou', he looks up at me, his face softening, as if no one else calls him that.

"And," I add, "with a better roof!"

He laughs. "You're on, Nirvana! I'll think about where."

I smile back, but then we're both a bit flat again. We've all but lost one of our few afternoons, and it seems a long time till tomorrow.

He suddenly looks away from the whiteout in front of us and at me. "Another idea..."

"Yes?" My heart leaps.

"The night we met, you escaped somehow..."

I can hardly stop my grin forming. He's had the self-same thought.

I nod. "It's easy. My bedroom opens onto the balcony."

"Tonight then, shall we go to Chalet Ouzon? To see the shepherd's table?"

I feel the huge grin spread over my face.

81

"Let's do it!" I say in English. "I could come out by…eleven?"

"It's a hard walk, Nirvana. We will need snowshoes because the snow will be deep. That okay?"

"I don't have any," I admit, though nothing, bar nothing, is going to stop me going.

"I'll bring my mother's." He sniffs. "You just need to wear walking or snow boots. I'll bring some food. I'm always hungry."

I smile. "So, we meet here, as usual?" Where our igloo once was.

"No, at the ski racks. We're going quite a way up Mont Ouzon." He points towards the mountain opposite, the scalloped one he showed me on Christmas Eve.

"Great!" I can think of nothing more exciting. "But now I really must go."

"See you soon!" he says.

No need for *tomorrows* this time.

THIRTEEN

WHAT SEEMED A catastrophe is now working to our advantage, I realise, as I review the blueprint for my miner's table at my desk. Ghislaine's demolition project has catalysed us into going to the farm tonight; tomorrow, we'll create the best igloo ever because we'll be building it together.

But I do need to talk to Sab about what's happened.

> **NIV: No igloo to shelter in anymore— demolished.**
>
> *Typing...*

It rarely takes Sab long to reply.

> *SAB: Big bad wolf? A right Three Pigs situation!*

She's the only person who could make me laugh about it! Though the comparison is an insult to wolves.

> **NIV: That Ghislaine again.**
>
> *SAB: ????????? seriously, I don't get it—her.*
>
> NIV: You and me both.

SAB: So what you gonna do?

NIV: Rebuild job. Somewhere she can't find.

I don't tell her about our plans for tonight though. I'm scared of jinxing it because if Mum or Dominique catch me escaping, it's over before it's even started.

OVER TEA, I have to work really hard at covering up my excitement. To tone it down, I play *Escape from Colditz* from the chalet's game chest with Mum and Dominique. My crowning moment is when I get the Rolls Royce card, which means I get to drive out of the prisoner-of-war camp right under their Nazi noses!

After my victory, I get my PJs on so I at least look like I'm going to bed but leave my shutters open so they won't creak when it's time to creep out.

At ten-thirty, I sneak into the hall and lounge, checking Mum and Dominique are both in bed. They sleep so soundly after skiing, I can hear their steady breathing through the gap in their door. I don't care if I'm early at the ski racks; I can't wait any longer. My backpack's all ready, with water, my tape measure and some chocolate for Jean-Lou.

GETTING OUT MY window's easier second time around. I stand for a moment on the balcony. It's not the clear night of Christmas Eve, but the snow's falling thinly and gently, as if the clouds are finally running out of enthusiasm for it.

I stride out through the empty village to the ski racks hoping to be there first and maybe see where he lives. But he's there before me, already wearing huge snowshoes that look like someone's drawn around your boots with a massive margin. The theory is, the bigger surface area means you walk on top of deep snow instead of through it.

"*Salut!*" he whispers a little shyly. "*Ça va?*"

I nod, too excited to speak.

He lays the snowshoes out on the car park, and I step my right foot onto one and stoop to fasten the straps. I can do the one across the front of my foot. The ankle's trickier as you have to twist around on one leg.

Jean-Lou kneels on the ground to help. Almost falling over, I make a grab his shoulder.

"Sorry," I murmur, letting go.

"S'okay," he says. "I'll do the other side too."

I'm a strange mix of chuffed and embarrassed to have him looking after me like this. I have to stop myself wondering, hoping about what it might mean.

As I take my first steps, I almost fall forward, as the plastic shoes feel like they grind through the thin layer of snow into the surface of the car park, which was snowploughed earlier.

Jean-Lou takes my arm. "It will become easier as we come to deeper snow."

The bases flap up against my boots like giants' flip-flops as we walk side by side along the car park till we're level with the blue piste. His hand slips down my arm to take my gloved hand, even though I don't really need it now. We cross the road to a track that starts directly opposite and winds back on itself till it reaches the rear of the chalets behind ours. From there, it ascends steeply, much more sharply than the path up to where our igloo was. Soon, we enter a pine wood, whose trees seem to stand back like friendly spectators as we pass between them. I want to tell Jean-Lou that, but I'm having to focus so hard on keeping up, I can't speak.

Eventually, we emerge from the wood, onto an open corner where I have to stop, just for a moment. Only now does he release my hand. I stretch it out—it's actually stopped snowing completely.

"*Ça va*, Nirvana?"

I nod, not wanting to give away how breathless I am.

"It's less steep from here."

As we walk, he tells me how his grandfather inherited the little chalet from his father, who was born at the end of the nineteenth century, I think he said.

Then he stops and thumbs his phone. "Yep, still a signal here, but not for much longer." He shows me a picture of the Alpine cows they kept high on the meadows of Mont Ouzon.

"So beautiful!" I exclaim. They're all soft cream and caramel with wide, gentle eyes and big bells around their necks, nothing like the stark black-and-white Friesians we have at home.

"You should see the Alps in the spring and summer, Nirvana. It's a different world. You know Alp means 'high pasture'? And they are full of flowers as well as cows! Plus, there are lakes where you can swim."

Nothing I'd like more than to see all that, I think, *and to swim with you in mountain lakes, however cold they are.*

Like that's ever going to happen!

The further we get from the ski station, the better.

"So, your grandfather and father grew up on this farm?" I ask as I step gingerly over a snow-clad cattlegrid.

"It's a bit more complicated than that. Where we go to now, is not actually a farm. As well as the small chalet, there is a milking shed. The farm was down in Le Biot."

We bought cheese there on our way from the airport.

"That's where they lived during the winter, with their cows under their living area. The chalet not far above us now is where they lived in the summer. The cows always stayed outside then," he adds, a smile in his voice.

The track has opened out into such wide curves now that we can see ahead of us because yes! The Moon has found a chink through the clouds, which finally seem to have emptied out all their snow.

Once we've rounded the elbow, we start to climb more steeply again. The track's sheltered from snow here, so stones catch on the bases of my snowshoes.

And there! All at once, the top of the chalet appears on a small plateau above us.

As we get nearer, it's clear how different a traditional Alpine chalet is from the one Dominique's rented for this week. Its timbers are vertical for one thing, and even in the moonlight, I can tell it's almost black with age. The windows are small, to keep in the heat, I suppose.

"The cheese store," Jean-Lou says as we pass a small, stone version of a cupboard built into the rock to our right.

"Like their fridge?"

"Well, yes, but only for cheese. They made it here, of course, during the summer—the main purpose of the cows."

Next, we pass the milking shed, built into the side of the slope on which the chalet sits. Soon, we're on the level area in front of where three generations of his family have lived.

We stand for a moment to look back at where we've come from. The clouds are straggly enough now to see the whole top half of the ski station, spanning from Toblerone Mountain to our left, across the round-shouldered one, and above it, the highest: la Pointe du Mont. Somewhere down in the dip of the valley is the village with our hopefully sleeping families; the site of our igloo. Behind us stands Mont Ouzon, broad and solid.

Just outside the door of Chalet Ouzon, identified by a wide wooden sign, we undo our snowshoes and Jean-Lou shrugs off his backpack. I light his way with my phone torch while he scrabbles for a key that turns out to be huge and jiggles it in the lock.

I have to try not to jiggle about too, with excitement.

FOURTEEN

I LINGER IN THE doorway while he fumbles around inside; he reappears in the glow of a lantern. I step into a small square room, and we stand together in the middle as I peer into the flickering shadows.

To the right of the door is a kitchen area with a stone sink, then two doors. Directly across from me is a closed shutter almost the whole width of the wall. That must give the same view we just had—of the mountains on the far side of the col. Diagonally opposite me, an open-fire range fills the whole corner with a couple of easy chairs, one either side of it; on the left-hand side is a pine dresser, and wooden skis decorate the wall. Those I wouldn't mind so much—Jean-Lou's family will have used them to get around or to have a bit of fun on open fields. What offends about the ski station is how it's scarred the landscape, pine forests felled for fast metal skis and the fastest, ugliest means back to the top to do it all again.

"This has...it has..." I start.

I can't find the words in French, so I just open my hands and beam at him instead. Though the air's freezing, the chalet has a warmth, a positive air, like it's known a lot of happiness.

"Take this a moment, Nirvana," he says, offering the lantern to me. I follow him towards the range, where he takes some kindling from a basket, stacks it in the grate and lights it from a box of matches, but the thin sticks soon fizzle out.

"Let me," I say, giving the lantern back to him.

I put another match to sticks, blow on the feeble flame and add some pinecones from the same basket so it flares.

"Logs?" I ask him.

He indicates a stack against the wall to my right. I pick some small ones with cut surfaces and add them to the cones.

"Thanks, Nirvana," he says as it blazes. "Now I'm really hungry. You?"

I'm not really, not after the amount of *bœuf bourguignon* I put away earlier, but I nod anyway. We've never eaten together before.

"Here it is," he says, taking the lantern towards the dresser.

Of course, the reason we came at all—the *table de berger*. It's like a set of shelves only boarded up, which is, of course, the table itself. Its pine is rich and heavy, the colour of toffee.

I reach up to twist the basic swivel catch. Then I turn to check with him I'm doing it right.

"Go ahead," he tells me.

Ready to support the weight of the table, I lower it gently down on its wide hinge from the dresser.

A leg topples out, and I crouch down to work out how to slot it into a rough square inset in the thick tabletop.

"I've sat at this so often with my dad," he tells me, "when we come up to stay in the summer."

I lean across it, smoothing my hand over the surface as I imagine two, three, four members of his family sitting around it. Once I've taken pictures of it from all angles, I get out my tape measure and record all the dimensions of the tabletop, leg and upright part in my notebook. Mine'll look quite different in oak, but it's still really helpful as a model.

Not wasting any more eating time, Jean-Lou rests his backpack on the table before extracting a baguette and a packet. We both get out our water bottles, and I pull out my Christmas Toblerone. I smile at him across the table; we're actually sharing a mini-meal by lantern and firelight at…twenty to one in the morning! And I completely get why he seems so at ease here, so totally content.

"This is the cheese my great-grandparents used to make, and which is still made in the region," he says, slicing a chunk off it with a penknife and holding it out to me on its point. "It's called Abondance, after our valley."

My mouth waters.

"Mmm." It's nutty and creamy. "And they made this here?"

He nods. "Right there!" He points. "Through that door are the steps leading to the milking room and the *fromagerie*."

The little room soon heats up. As Jean-Lou munches his way through more cheese on chunks of baguette, then mountain-shaped triangles of chocolate, I lean back in my solid pine chair and gaze at the open fire, feeling completely at home.

When he's finally eaten enough, he shows me the freezing *fromagerie* below with its wide stone sink and counter. We don't bother unlocking the door to the milking shed. Back upstairs, there are two more doors.

"This is where my uncle slept," he says, showing me a room almost filled by two single beds. "And my father, but only till he was four. Then my grandparents moved down into the village because it was too far for them to walk down and back to get the bus to the *école primaire* in Le Biot."

"And this was my grandparents' room," he says.

We stand in the doorway, looking at the small, double bed with one of those proper old-fashioned quilts and square French pillows. I could just fall sleep on it. But the image my imagination shoots up is of both of us, Jean-Lou and me, holding each other so close our heads share the same pillow.

Oh God! I blush hotly and have to bite my bottom lip to try to hide my thoughts. As I look at his warm eyes, his lips, his *beautiful* face, all the times we've had together in five short days light up my mind in a blaze of joyful colours. And I can't pretend to myself any longer.

Of course this is how I feel for Jean-Lou.

"What?" he asks quietly, as my eyes are still on him.

I shake my head, still adjusting to how, from over a thousand miles away, Sab intuited what I couldn't even dare to admit to myself. Because really, what are the chances of someone like him being interested in someone like me?

92

Smiling a little, he's still looking at me for some sort of answer.

"I wish…" I hesitate, scared of letting on too much.

He nods for me to go on.

"I wish we could stay here." My face heats up again.

After a pause, he nods, his dimple flickering like he's guessed my feelings. "Maybe one night."

But how? When? I only have two more nights left. What's he thinking? Or is he just a dreamer?

Jean-Lou closes the bedroom door behind us. "Time to go?"

I sigh. But we must go, I suppose.

He puts out the fire while I fold the table back upright and clip it into place.

My first and last time here, I think as he locks the door behind us and zips away the key.

I BEND TO put on my snowshoes, which we've left outside the door.

"We don't need these yet," Jean-Lou tells me.

Not far back down the mountain, at the wide, open bend, he stops and pulls off his backpack.

"Shortcut," he says, pulling two folded pieces of plastic from his backpack.

Pan sledges, just big enough for your bum!

"We start here," he says at the top of the snowfield filling in the V of the elbow, "and it's the first to the bottom."

"Not fair!" I say, sitting on the plastic anyway. "You're heavier than me."

"Then I'll give you a few seconds' start," he says. "But I'll still win! You go at three, I go at—"

"Twenty."

"Ten," he says firmly.

Laughing, I don't wait for his count but, holding onto the plastic handle at the front, push off with my feet. Once I'm launched, I stick my legs out in front of me. As the ground gets steeper, I shriek. No control!

Jean-Lou streaks past me, his victory shout snatched away with him.

But then he veers off to the side, into the elbow instead of straight down. I'm the first to the bottom and come to a stop in a heap of snow that finds its way down my neck.

Panting, I lie on my back and gaze up at the glittering sky.

"The best one won," Jean-Lou admits, smiling as he comes and stands over me.

"The prize?" I ask breathlessly.

He holds out his gloved hand to tug me out of the drift.

"The prize is this beautiful night, Nirvana," he says, serious for a second as I stand in front of him. Close.

"That's the best prize ever," I murmur, looking up at him. "Thank you, Jean-Lou."

So then? The perfect moment for my first ever kiss? Our first kiss…

But he doesn't bend his head. The moment's gone. We drop hands, and gutted, I stumble away in the deep snow to retrieve my sledge.

This time, I perch on a snow drift to attach the *raquettes* myself.

As we march back down the hill, neither of us saying a word, I get colder and colder. I'm flat, grey inside. He clearly doesn't feel *that* way for me. I didn't fully know till tonight how much I wanted him to kiss me. But it looks like all his smiling, all his attention, suggesting meetings, holding my hand earlier, was just him being friendly and helpful.

"It was one of the best nights of my life," I tell him anyway, as I give the snowshoes back to him near the ski racks.

"For me too," he says quietly, raising my hopes all over again.

So why don't we kiss? I can't drag myself away from him, even though I'm knackered and freezing. Maybe he didn't kiss me up the mountain because he was too uncertain of my reaction. It'd be friggin' awful to get back to England and never know if...

What've I got to lose? Other than face.

I look at his lips, which so fascinate me, I *have* to feel them on mine. I'm about to reach up on my toes when he opens his mouth to speak.

"So, Nirvana, we build our new igloo later today?"

I nod, trying to hide my disappointment. "See you later."

As I TRUDGE back to the chalet, I'm all shrunken inside. What a fool am I! He stopped me just in time. Before I ruined the few happy times we've got left. Why *should* he fancy me? I'm nothing special. Nothing special at all.

All French collèges are mixed, and the way he looks, Jean-Lou will be surrounded by girls far more intelligent and attractive than me. Girls he can have an ongoing relationship with. We've got on really well really quickly. He's a great listener, and we have some unforgettable times. I should make the most of us being just good friends while I can.

What do I tell Sab now? I think, finally in bed.

No Romeo for *this* Juliet.

FIFTEEN

I T SEEMS NO time at all till I'm back at the ski racks. I left a note by the kettle last night saying, quite truthfully, I hadn't got to sleep till extremely late and to let me sleep in. But it's been long enough to come to terms with the fact that there's nothing romantic between us. Now I'm just dead set on making the most of every unique, magical second with Jean-Lou.

"Hi, Nirvana!" he says, emerging from the Groundhog Day murk. He sounds just as excited as me about our new igloo. He glances at my feet. "Great, you're ready."

The mood's all frothy between us again as he leads us along the car park in the opposite direction from last night, in front of the resto. He seems so happy, I allow myself to hope he might have some feelings for me but is too sensible, too caring even for some sort of fling that can't have a future.

As we pass its front path, cleared yet again by poor Monsieur Gilbert, I suppose, the door bangs and heavy steps clonk down the path.

"*Hé!*" a voice says.

A voice I recognise. Hers. Our nemesis.

Jean-Lou's in front of me now and doesn't seem to have heard. So I stop.

Pulse speeding, I pivot around and stride back to the path. I've no idea what she wanted to say to Jean-Lou— or me. It can't be anything either of us wants to hear, but I've got something to say to her. As I march towards her, I'm trying to decide what to choose out of all the words storming my mind.

When I'm within hearing distance, I get in first.

"Was it you who destroyed our igloo?"

Her eyes hold mine, won't let them go. Almost inhuman. Jean-Lou's 'monster' echoes in my mind.

"And?" she says.

I cough a gasp at her one word of admission.

"But...why?" I stutter.

"Why not?" she says, still keeping eye contact.

"Because...because it was ours."

She shrugs. "*Tant pis.*"

Too bad, her few words taunting me, as if I'm not worth more.

"What are you anyway?" she says scathingly. "*Petits enfants?*"

"Nirvana!" Jean-Lou calls me from just down the path. I half turn to him.

"Nirvana, is it?" she sneers. I hate my name in her mouth. It sounds all wrong.

"Leave it, please," he says, nearer now.

"Well, Nirvana, you need to know, he is a complete waste of time."

I've never felt as gobsmacked, never so totally disorientated by an exchange. I turn to go, to Jean-Lou. But then I halt on the path. He actually strides towards me and reaches out to stop me going back. I shake my

98

head at him, stalk back, all these words rushing into my mouth, words I can only say in English.

"I don't know what your game is," I tell her, "but it's ridiculous. I have no idea who or...*what* you are..."

She smirks at me, understanding the tone if not the meaning.

I gather myself up and find my French at last. "The only waste of time here is you. You do not even do your job. While Jean-Louis is the kindest and most interesting person I have ever met."

Now I TURN and go to him. He's waiting, head down, at the bottom of the path.

We walk, fast, towards Toblerone Wood, neither of us able to speak.

I have to almost run to keep up with his pace. Simultaneously, I'm both trying to erase what just happened because she's not worth it and work out what the frigg is going on.

When Jean-Lou finally stops at the entrance to the wood, some of it bursts out of me.

"My God, Jean-Lou, I've never met anyone like that in my life. She's...not normal."

He's studying the snow. "I wish you'd not talked to her, Nirvana," he says quietly. "She wants a reaction. You can't win with her."

"But why? Of course you can. She cannot get away with everything."

I can't think of the French for it, but I think he understands what I mean.

"Why would she want to turn me against you?" I ask him.

A supposed adult, too. Though in fact, I don't feel like I was talking to a human at all. Those eyes are branded in my memory.

"Thank you for…fighting for me," he says, looking to the side of my face now, his lips in a rigid line, "but you don't understand."

He strides off again, deeper into the woods.

I stand and stare after him for a moment, then I run. I run right around in front of him. All the light's gone out of Jean-Lou, and he's in a far worse state than when our igloo was destroyed.

Without thinking, I grab both his hands. Even through our padded gloves, I can feel them shaking. I grip his hands tighter.

"Then help me to understand," I tell him.

The pines' heavy, outstretched arms meet over our heads, sheltering us from the icy wind and the worst of the snow.

We're here, they whisper to me, *it'll be all right.*

"It'll be all right," I pass on to Jean-Lou.

He looks at me.

"She's trying to keep her control," he says, then hesitates. "She can see I'm happy when I'm with you. So she wants to spoil that."

Only dimly aware of what this means for us, I shake my head. "But why? What's it got to do with her?"

His Adam's apple shifts as he takes a big swallow.

"She's my mother."

SIXTEEN

GHISLAINE IS JEAN-LOU'S *mother?*
    I open my mouth. Close it again before the wrong words come out.

She can't be.

How can someone so bitter be the mother of someone who smiles and loves life so much?

Yet somewhere deep inside me, I've also always known.

I keep tight hold of his hands as, gazing into the trees, images of her replay in my mind, in each of them, those dead eyes.

Smoking in the resto.

Letting me flounder in the snow as metal discs whizzed past my head.

Annihilating our igloo.

Only now do I get it. The knocking down of our igloo was a knocking down of *him.* What kind of mother would do that?

Jean-Lou's eyes are cast towards the ground, and there's a tightness in his mouth. Maybe this is something he's not talked about before?

I'm blocking him in, trapping him, I suddenly realise.

"Let's walk, Jean-Lou, shall we?"

I don't want to let go of him, but I'm going to have to.

We walk slowly under the white arms reaching over our heads, still shielding us.

"Why is she like this?" I ask.

"It's taken me years and years to understand her," he says at last.

The thought of him trying to figure her out as a little lad...I want to take his hand again.

"Her bitterness, it's got two reasons. The first's obvious. She hates being stuck in the mountains."

I can kind of understand that. Even though Jean-Lou's helped me learn to *adore* it, it's so remote and limited if you don't actually love the climate or appreciate its beauty. Why then wouldn't they consider moving as a family, maybe somewhere still near enough the mountains for his dad and him?

"The other is..." He pauses, and I find myself holding my breath. "Me."

"You? How can it be you, Jean-Lou?" I've never heard anything so ridiculous. "You, you're...*parfaitement bien*."

Then I feel a right idiot. *Just right* is a phrase I've lifted from Claude's *Goldilocks* story book in French!

Jean-Louis stops and turns to me, his dimple hovering for the first time since my set-to with *her*.

"Well," I say, blushing, "you are!"

Now he blushes and starts walking again but times his steps so I can walk next to him.

"She never wanted children," he says after a long moment.

I reel inside at the contrast with all Mum and Dominique went through to have me and Claude.

"As a little child, she never even allowed me to call her *maman*. Only Ghislaine," he tells me.

That ugly name suits her perfectly, I think, my blood buzzing with disgust. I can't stop myself; I put my arm through his. He doesn't look at me, but he does loop his to hold mine in place.

"*Grand-mère*, Papa's mother," he goes on, "helped me understand things a bit before she died. She explained how my mother felt I had come between her and my father. But then, because she was so...cold towards me, it was Papa and I who became close instead."

This puzzles me. I've heard of mothers who can't bond with their babies at first, before they grow to love them, but this...this is something else.

"And now she can't wait to be rid of me next year. To some job. She won't have me going to university then coming home at the end of each semester. I have to work all year round. Not just help at the resto in the holidays and cost them money the rest of the year. I must be gone."

I find myself shaking my head as we walk. "But it doesn't mean she and your dad will suddenly be happy again."

"I think she hopes Papa will finally agree to move when it's no longer two of us who want to stay here. But he won't. He and his family have always lived here. But more than this, he has no...incentive to want to please her."

"Does he...does he know what she's like?"

He shakes his head. "She's very clever at hiding the worst of it." He shrugs. "And I can hardly tell tales about the things she does."

I know exactly what he means because that's how I felt on Christmas morning. It's hard to put into words how wrong her behaviour was without sounding petty.

"All I can do," he says, "is avoid being alone with her. Such as when Papa is working in the resto and she's in the apartment."

Hence our igloo.

We can see the light at the end of this filigree tunnel of trees now. So many thoughts are flashing around my brain, I don't know what to say to help him.

"I think you've maybe spoken with him, my father?" he says.

I frown. How's that possible?

"At the resto," he explains.

I shake my head. "But he's Monsieur Gilbert."

Jean-Lou smiles. "Gilbert is his first name! Gilbert Jaboulay."

"He's…you're…" I'm burbling in English. I catch my breath. "So your father owns the resto? And he's married to…"

No wonder his dad sometimes looks so forlorn! And no wonder he couldn't stop her smoking inside. He's such a lovely man, it makes sense that it's rubbed off on his son, and he's been strong enough to build Jean-Lou up, give him the strength to be himself.

As we step out of the shelter of the woods, a broad field of snow falls gently away below us. Its huge, white expanse is dazzlingly, excitingly blank. A new page.

"Jean-Lou," I say quietly, "you could've told me, you know. Who she was." *Maybe when she let me fall off the lift-pull or destroyed our igloo.* "It changes nothing about you." *Or between us.*

He turns to me, his eyes finally meeting mine. "Thank you, Nirvana."

"And I'm certain..." I begin, then hesitate.

"You can say what you think with me, Nirvana. Always."

"I am certain, from what I know of you, one caring parent is enough to help create a...marvellous person."

Now he smiles properly.

"Come on!" he says. "We've an igloo to build. This way!" He takes a sharp right up a steep track which intersects a further part of the forest.

I have to work at keeping up as he strides out. This is *our* time now. We have so little left, today and ever.

Two more nights then home.

My heart aches and aches.

Soon, he stops and turns left along a narrow animal track deep into the trees. Now even he has to use his phone torch to light our way through the dark forest.

We walk horizontally, more or less.

At one point, a fallen tree blocks our way.

We stride over it and continue single file along the animal track. Finally, he stops and holds back a branch for me.

"Wow!" My voice is muffled by all the pines and snow.

It's a clearing, not unlike my woodland workshop at home. At this height, though, it's a mini plateau.

Smiling at me, Jean-Lou produces a folding spade out of his backpack.

"You must show me how to build this better roof you talked of!" he teases.

I smile back at him as I use the spade's edge to draw the outline of our base right in the middle of the plateau. The return of his happiness has made me realise: what we're doing now is not only rebuilding an igloo his mother demolished, but Jean-Lou too.

We agree the entrance should point away from the path we came on for even more privacy, and it should be a little bigger than the first one—higher with a longer tunnel, to accommodate Jean-Lou's size. He's already rolling snowballs into hard snow that can then be shaped into blocks.

I do a prototype of each size of brick we'll need, and it's hard work; so much so I'm soon sweating under my thermals.

When we have enough base blocks, we start to build.

We're both hard at it, no time for chat beyond brief exchanges of words: time's against us, and we can't leave it roofless in this snow. Yet magic hovers in this glade. We seem so remote from everyone else that nothing's on my mind but building.

Rebuilding Jean-Lou, stronger, together.

"A work of art!" he declares quite some time later as we stand back to view it from a little distance.

It is truly beautiful. Because the blocks are freshly hewn, their perimeters are visible in a way they never will be again, just like you'd see in a cartoon igloo. Perfect.

"And no one will ever find it," I tell him.

We'll be completely alone, completely safe here.

We both take its photo.

I check my tracker: even though I have longer now Claude's with our parents, we haven't time to sit in it, only poke our heads inside.

"I don't want to leave it now," I moan. "What if we just stay here?"

Away from his monster mother.

"Then we'd get very hungry," he says, starting to head off out of the clearing, "and zhe game is up," he ends in English.

I smile a little. "You did find out the meaning."

And he's using it to console me about having to leave our igloo, I realise, as we approach the fallen tree. But I can't forget tomorrow is my last full day here. That tightness reappears in my gullet.

"Why am I only ever free for tiny pieces of time," I ask, "always having to watch the clock?"

He gives me a sympathetic mouth shrug. "Montaigne would say this is what happens when we are part of man-made society, whereas, inside us, we know what is perfect."

We look at each other, then I twist back towards our gorgeous clearing.

I nod. "Nature. So let's go back, Jean-Lou, stay in nature at our igloo!" I grin. "I'll carve a spear out of a stick. Hunt for rabbits. Make a fire! We can melt ice to drink."

"A free spirit as well as a druid!" His smiley, shining eyes tell me he'd love it too.

"It's just..." I shrug, more serious now. "We have so little time with our new igloo. I'm going home the day after tomorrow."

Only two nights to go.

A pause.

"That's come very fast."

The waver in his voice makes my throat tight but also gives me new hope. Maybe I'm not just a diversion.

"Sometimes we've got to give up a little freedom in order to have more freedom," he says, his dimple suggesting something more.

"Who said that?"

"Me!" His face lights up. "Because tonight, Nirvana, we can be completely free!"

"We can?" My pulse speeds up.

"If you can escape again?"

I nod, beaming.

"So let's meet at the entrance to the little wood, our usual time."

Our usual time! My pulse dances with pleasure.

Now I know. He wants to see me as much as I do him.

SEVENTEEN

As I trudge back up to the chalet, I'm all *bouleversée*—shaken upside down, like a miniature person inside my own snow globe. I can't wait for tonight, to be in our new igloo no one will ever find. Nothing, bar nothing, could be better.

But once I've gone home, Jean-Lou will still be stuck with her, Ghislaine. No wonder he wouldn't want to swap mums! I'm unravelling the last five days in my mind: Christmas Eve afternoon, he must have been avoiding her. If his dad was working in the resto and she wasn't working on the pistes that day, they would otherwise have been stuck in their apartment together. Urggh!

The afternoons, though, could they possibly have been about just seeing me?

Veering from horror to guiltily hugging myself about tonight, I climb the steps to the chalet.

CLAUDE'S RAVE ABOUT slaloming while we eat risotto for tea seems a long way away from my secret life with Jean-Lou, though I try to nod now and again. I glance across the table at my mums and remember clearly all they had to go through to get Claude.

Gay couples never stumble into a baby, of course. It took over two years for Mum and Dominique to 'start' Claude, for Mum to be able to carry Dominique's egg.

Still, I can imagine how tough it must be to find yourself pregnant unexpectedly and unhappily. Yet Ghislaine had, *has*, a responsibility to the life she helped create. Isn't a baby always good news once it's born, once you see him, know him as a real person? Maybe not if you're in a terrible situation, but Jean-Lou's mother wasn't on her own or in poverty. It feels to me like she wouldn't even allow herself the chance to *learn* to love Jean-Lou as he grew up. And in not doing, she's lost her marriage anyway.

The apple's certainly fallen far from *that* tree.

And how strange, that the one most like Cal is not me, with my missing parent, but Jean-Lou and his monster mother right here and now! At least Cal's mother left them in peace, whereas Ghislaine Jaboulay keeps Jean-Lou and his dad in an ongoing purgatory. The eighteen months till Jean-Lou leaves home is a long time when she must make him unhappy every day.

"More salad, Nirvan-ah?" Dominique asks. "Ça va— you are very quiet?" she says as she puts more on my plate.

I smile at her, nodding as I remember just how lucky I am. At least *my* parents' efforts at controlling means they care.

When I've helped clear up, I go to my room. Lying on my bed, I can't stop thinking about Jean-Lou. The way it all spilled out of him, it seemed like now his grandmother has gone, he has no one to talk to about it anymore.

He is clear it's a problem with his mother, not him, isn't he? My heart hurts that he might think if he'd been different, she would have loved him. What can I say or do to help?

I glance at my phone and wonder whether I'd feel better if I just told Sab about it all. But I'm not sure even she could offer advice on this one.

Mum would know, with her psychologist/counselling hat on. We've had a sort of avoiding-the-subject truce since our big difference of opinion. If she thinks I'm backing down, though, she couldn't be more wrong: Jean-Lou's support just reinforces my determination to do an apprenticeship.

But I'm sure Mum could help me understand Jean-Lou's mother a little more. And that'd be huge because as things are, Ghislaine's very real.

And hurting Jean-Lou.

CLAUDE'S ROOM'S ALL quiet. Dominique's mopping up after his bathtime. I find Mum washing up. My heart jolts at the chance, though I'm aware things are still strained between us as I pick up a tea towel.

"I need to ask you a...strange question, Mum."

"I'll do my best," she says, putting a plate on the draining board.

I take a deep breath. "If someone had a baby by accident, even if they were married, could it be hard to love that baby? And could the mother resent it for coming between her and her husband?"

She turns to me, her face a puzzle.

"It relates to my Lit novel," I bluster, trying not to lie outright.

Her expression relaxes and she turns back to the sink, scrubbing the casserole dish.

"Well, that situation is the opposite of my experience, Niv, because I wanted you more than anything even though I had no partner at the time, only your grandparents. And Claude was also very much wanted— you saw how much effort it took for Dominique and me to have him. But…"

She puts the dish on the drainer and turns to lean back against the sink, obviously thinking.

"One thing psychology has taught me is, there's always some nugget of common ground between others' lives and our own. Take Claude, for instance…"

We both grin at the force of nature he is.

She nods. "There you go. He couldn't have had a bigger impact on our family's lives, could he? And you, love, you had no choice in him. We didn't ask your permission. I'm not asking how you felt then…"

I bite my top lip because I *did* feel jealous. I tried to hide it because what good what would it have done to show it? At nine, I was pretty independent, but first I'd had to share Mum with Dominique and then with a new baby who wasn't even biologically related to me. Or my mum.

And yet…

"I think I know how you feel now," Mum says.

I nod. Once I got to know Claude, understand his funny ways, it was impossible not to love him.

She smiles her lovely smile, her hair soft around her face. "Love expands, doesn't it? It has no limits."

"Yeah, so what does that say for mothers like Cal's?"

For Jean-Lou's.

She shrugs a little. "I think it's natural for love to take time for some mothers and fathers."

"But for it *never* to come?"

She turns back to the sink and pulls the plug, draining away the dirty water.

"There will be different reasons," she says as she runs a brush around the sink and I finish the drying, "but it sounds to me something like the narcissistic personality trait. Narcissists can't really love anyone, not properly. They love themselves too much. So if they have children, possibly against their wishes, they have no primal instincts for them. The child becomes more of something they can choose to do with as they wish."

A shiver runs through me. That sounds exactly like Ghislaine.

"Is it something you just can't help then? Steinbeck said Cal's mother was just born a monster?"

Her lips puff out a long breath as she dries her hands. "It's a much-debated subject. Experts are divided on how much these disorders are inherited and how much down to their upbringing and circumstances."

"But what do *you* think, Mum?" I persist.

She's quiet for a moment, gazing past me as she ponders before bringing her eyes back to me. "What I think is, people have a predisposition towards being a certain way. Then something in their environment can trigger or exacerbate it. Nature through nurture."

I nod, trying to take this in and what it means for Jean-Lou.

"Do you think one of these narcissists could ever change?"

She blows out. "Tough questions tonight, Niv! Maybe, but they would have to struggle hard against their syndrome. So even if they could, it is perhaps not very common that they would. Even then, I suspect it'd be learnt rather than felt behaviour—they'd be going through the motions."

This is sounding pretty hopeless for Jean-Lou.

I take a big breath. "My very last question, Mum." The most important of all. "Can a child of one of these narcissistic people survive? Be happy?"

"You seem to be very interested in the psychology of this story, Niv," she says, a question in her tone.

"I want to know what sort of future the main character has after the story ends," I tell her, ignoring how surprised she is to see me apparently so into a book.

"Well, my feeling is, they certainly can. Especially if they have one good parent who loves them."

I nod in relief: that's more or less what I said to Jean-Lou, on instinct.

"Cal has a good father," I tell her as I turn off the kitchen light and follow her into the lounge, where I put another log on the burner.

"You know, Niv, you could consider taking psychology as one of your A' levels."

Friggin' A' levels—*again*! My stomach tenses. She actually thinks she won that argument?!

Knocked for six, I sit back on my heels, trying to screen the words about to erupt from my mouth. Apart from having to keep Jean-Lou from her, it's been so

114

good talking to Mum tonight, like how we used to be. Now she's wiped it out in one sentence.

I straighten up and turn to her, trying to keep my voice level.

"Not doing A' levels doesn't mean I'm stupid, you know. I'm still interested in loads of stuff. I just want to *live* life, not read and write about it. You've just been talking about predispositions, Mum. Why can't you accept mine is to create and build."

She sighs. "I don't think woodwork is actually genetically wired in you, Niv!"

I feel my shoulders hunch up to my ears.

"Why not?" Joinery *could* be an aptitude from my donor dad. "It *feels* built in," I tell her. "And I don't want to struggle against what I love doing. Which is a really worthwhile and important thing to do, actually. I don't want to give it up for some qualifications that would only make me unhappy."

There's a movement in the doorway. How long has Dominique been there?

"I am not ganging up on you, Nirvan-ah," she says in French. "I simply want to make this point. Over half of English teenagers study for A' levels. If you *can* do them, you need a very good reason not to."

"And I've just given it," I tell her. "My happiness."

EIGHTEEN

WHEN I OPEN my window, I can't be anything other than happy! I catch my breath at the Moon, brighter even than Christmas Eve; so bright, it's almost daylight! The pines are giants once more against the white sheet of ski pistes, the silhouettes of all the mountains as clear as scenery under stage lights, and above the Toblerone Mountain and Bear Mountain a smattering of stars. Gleaming and sharp, they leave no room for clouds. It's clearer than I've *ever* seen *any* night sky.

All is hushed outside, but I can't stop my boots crunching in the frozen snow as I hurry down the road in front of the sleeping chalets. There's no sign of Jean-Lou in the village, but as I get closer to Toblerone Wood, I see him, waiting at its entrance. The night's so silent, we whisper quick, smiley greetings.

The wood really is magical in the moonlight. The white arms of the tall firs throw shadows like palm branches in front of us. At first, it seems the crackle of our steps in the crusted snow is ruining the silence, but when we stop, deep among the trees, it turns out the night woods are so alive with rustlings of their own that you expect to see the gleaming eyes of rabbits, badgers, wild boar. That doesn't spook me: they wish us no harm and have every right to watch us romping through their home.

As we continue, all my senses are alert—the frosty purity of the night air on my skin, the fresh, almost sterile smell—and all around Jean-Lou and me, the atmosphere is charged with excitement and anticipation.

At the end of the wood, the broad piste by day has reverted to its natural state, a huge meadow of snow. Beyond and above it stands a whole set of toothy mountains that weren't visible this afternoon. I can't take my eyes off their jagged outline under the starry sky. It seems the mountains find their freedom at night too, another kindly presence sharing this glorious night with us.

As we take the steep track up to the right, the dense trees block out much of the moonlight. Once we take the sharp turn into the woods that are home to our new igloo, Jean-Lou has to use his big torch.

Over the fallen tree, on a little further and we're there!

OUR IGLOO'S SPOTLIT by the Moon, on a stage-in-the-round with an audience of trees.

I just stand and gaze.

This is all and only for us!

"Come on!" he says.

I go in first.

Jean-Lou scans a beam all around our igloo.

"Top job," I tell him in English.

He turns off his big torch. Snug and warm, we sit in the dark for so long, just listening to the deep, deep silence, taking in the snow's pure scent.

No one else in the whole world knows we're here.

Except an owl, his mellow, woody hoot tells us.

We both laugh.

After that, we don't talk again. Nothing needs to be said. We just are. Montaigne would be proud of us.

"Can we try something?" Jean-Lou says after a while.

We scramble back out into the clearing and, with a lot of manoeuvring, get our feet and legs back in the igloo so we can lie on our backs and gaze up at the night sky, gloved hands behind our heads to keep them off the snow.

We don't try to work out shapes, constellations. We just watch. Sometimes clouds veil the Moon, then drift airily on.

It does make me feel small but very alive too. We are of no significance at all, yet we are still part of this night. We came from stars; we will return to them. Our troubles with our parents, mine and even Jean-Lou's, they will pass. And the universe will go on.

"Whoa!" I say and grab his arm. "A shooting star."

No idea of the French.

"*Étoile filante*?" he says. "I missed it."

So, we lie and wait for another.

"Ptolemy said, when we see a shooting star," he tells me, "it's because the gods have opened up a crack in the heavens to look down at us. When a star falls through then you can ask the gods for something you want."

We scoff in unison.

"But what would you wish for?" I ask him, curious all the same.

He props himself up on his elbow to look at me through the moonlight.

"*Toi*," he whispers, "Nirvana."

My heart scrunches. Blooms.

"You already have your wish, Jean-Lou," I whisper back.

His nose is cold against mine. His lips warm, soft, light. They linger on mine and it's as if he's distilling everything he feels for me.

"Mmm," I murmur.

Yes to this delicious kiss. Yes to him. Yes to us.

Then our lips move, like the pause was a comma in a much longer sentence. He tastes fresh, piney, and he's totally focused on me, telling me how he feels.

I love being here with you, his lips tell me.

Me too, mine reply.

This current, I feel it fizzing through my blood.

The current passes between us, joining us.

Slowly, gently, we stop, the sentence finally coming to an end. He rests down from his elbow, turns so our faces are still so close. I knew his lips would be amazing!

"So, this is what a kiss is?" I murmur to him. "Saying things without even having to speak."

"I don't know other kisses. That is what *our* kiss is."

"Will it...will it be like that every time, Jean-Lou?"

He laughs. "I guarantee it, *ma Nirvana*!"

He says it like I really am his ultimate bliss! I love my name in his mouth. Always have, I now realise. And when he kisses me again, his hand drawing my head closer still, my heart's as big and light as a helium balloon.

When we kiss, we kiss...

"When did you first...feel this?" I ask. That he wanted me to be his Nirvana!

"Right from when you tried to claim rights to my igloo!"

I nudge him. "*My* igloo!"

He nudges me back.

"So what took you so long?"

He hesitates, and I get it, just too late.

"I didn't want any...thing to stop us."

Anyone more like. His friggin' mother. But yesterday he had to reveal who she was.

As if I'd let her get in our way! As if I'd let *anything* get in our way! I want to tell him, but I don't want him to think about her for even one second tonight.

"I didn't dare even to let myself hope till last night at Chalet Ouzon," I tell him instead. "But honestly, it was really the first ever time I saw this." Not knowing the French for it, I kiss the hollow of his dimple. "You are my best ever Christmas present, Jean-Lou."

He laughs. Then his thumb follows the shape of my full lower lip. Mum calls it pouty, but Nana said someone would want to kiss it one day. And here he is, kissing it.

My heart's giant. This is my Jean-Lou at his happiest. Because of me.

Finally, we're too cold to stay in the moonlight anymore.

In our igloo, his torch casting a candlelight glow, we kneel, holding each other so tight and close, our padded bodies fit together as we talk through our kisses.

When we're tired, we strip off our coats to make a bed, his underneath, mine on top, and sink down onto our sides, our knees interwoven.

"I'm worried, Jean-Lou, that you don't know who I really am."

"Because it is you, because it is I."

I smile to myself—he's actually been thinking about this thing between us, its inevitability.

"Montaigne?"

"Who else!"

"Who'd have thought it?" I say about the two of us, "A philosopher and a druid!"

"Perfect!" He laughs.

"But I still think you'll be disappointed if you get to know me better."

"Never," he says, running the backs of his fingers down my cheekbone. "The clearness of your skin, your eyes, this reflects who you are. Completely natural."

Only because I'm too lazy to be otherwise!

"You must know," he gives me a slow, light, tender kiss, "all that and your stunning hair, you're really beautiful, Nirvana."

I laugh. Even my hair! As if! But if he thinks I am, that's more than good enough for me.

"Jean-Lou, I'm just a very ordinary girl with loads of faults."

"It's not ordinary to be fierce for me, your oak tree, *ma petite druide*! To be determined for yourself."

I beam. "You, Jean-Lou, when I say you're *parfaitement bien,* I mean it. The way you look, the way you feel, but most of all, the way you are."

He kisses my pouty lip again.

"To me, you also are *parfaitement bien,* Nirvana, I promise you."

Maybe that's what falling for someone is. You see only the good in them. Still, we make a vow to each other: we will only ever tell each other the truth. About everything.

Because we're both completely new to it, we experiment, finding out kisses can also just be fun, nibbly and in different places, like my neck, which is beyond delicious. Then our kisses end up in long, involved ones, that current joining us and saying something. Jean-Lou's rhythm is slow and intense. His hand rubs me, smooths me, from my thigh over my hip and into the dip of my waist, finding the tender skin of my midriff under my fleece, making me ache in new places.

I feel excited and safe with him all at the same time.

"Do the French call this French kissing too?" I ask him, breathless.

He laughs. "I've never heard that. Sometimes it's called…" He hesitates. "Lovers' kissing."

"It—you—make me…wriggle," I finish in English.

"Is that good or not?" he asks, suddenly anxious. "What is it, this *wrigg-el*?"

I show him. "I think it means," I whisper, "my whole body wants to join in telling you things."

"Mine too," he whispers back.

Now I understand. This is what being lovers would be like. For us anyway. Not a separate thing from kissing; just a completely easy and natural continuation of what we've started. If only we can carry on some time…

We're lying flat on our backs, holding hands, my palms rougher than his, listening to the sound of silence again. My fingers are exploring his fingers, knuckles, wrist— a whole extra body to get to know. I've walked my fingers over his hard chest, felt the soft hairs in the middle; I know how his nose feels alongside mine, the graze of his upper lip, the softness of his hair.

"Can we do this again tomorrow night?" he asks.

"We must," I say, trying to keep my voice steady. "It's my last night."

He grips my hand tighter then turns onto his side to look at me.

"Then we have a New Year's party early, Nirvana." He kisses me. "One we'll never forget!"

NINETEEN

I WAKE UP IN deep black, my hip cold and aching along the side I'm lying on. We're still wrapped up in each other, meshed like two snowflakes, my face in his chest, under his chin.

I ease back in his arms, stroke his cheek. "Jean-Lou! We fell asleep!"

He doesn't stir. I actually have to shake him awake!

"Mm, Nirvana!" he says, as if I'm some wonderful surprise, and pulls me close again. He's all relaxed and supple, his long, slow kisses and touch coiling me up inside all over again.

Finally, I break away to grope for my phone. "We need to check the time."

It's almost six!

We sit bolt upright and, almost comically, flail around, falling into and over each other as we try to tug out our coats and squirm into them. His legs are so all over the place, we end up collapsing in a heap of laughter, me on top. I have to prise myself away from him again.

I CAN'T SLEEP when I get back, still in this state of euphoria at all that's just happened between us, reliving every magical moment from the appearance of the shooting star to waking up in his arms. Everything I wanted and more, much, much more. More than

I'd dared imagine. Last night, he must have been waiting for *the* perfect moment to kiss me!

We've become entwined in each other's lives in such a short time. I know from the few girls in our class who've had first kisses that they can be a complete let-down, even with someone you get on with. But with Jean-Lou and me, it felt so natural, so good!

It was the best night of my life. Part of me wants to keep it just between the two of us. But my joy's so overflowing, I long to tell Sab. Yep, even if she'll crow she knew it all along. I pick up my phone and scroll down the photos of our igloo 2.0 from yesterday afternoon and then in the moonlight. My heart pangs at the thought of sharing our gorgeous refuge with anyone. I just can't do it. I chew my lip and I wonder what to write instead. Once I've told her, I can't take it back. Will she be full of questions I don't want to answer? I just have to do it anyway—share the best ever night with my unique best friend.

NIV: First kisses with Jean-Louis last night.

A double tick says she's got the message, but there's no green sign of typing. Then, as my eyes are starting to close, a reply pings.

SAB: Yup.

Of course she's not surprised!

SAB: By the book?

I have to laugh. When we got to that bit in class, when Juliet says Romeo kisses by the book, Sab said it sounded like he was holding *Kissing for Dummies* over Juliet's shoulder! Miss had to explain it means Romeo kisses really well.

NIV: From the heart.

"YOU LOOK HAPPY," Dominique tells me a sleepless hour later. "I suppose it is because tomorrow we go home."

'Tomorrow' and 'home' stab at my heart. *One night to go.* She couldn't be more wrong.

"Don't want to go home," Claude says, folding his arms on the breakfast table.

Me neither. Not even for Rova and Grandad.

"You start preschool on Monday," Dominique reminds Claude. "You have been longing for that."

"Preschool!" he humphs. "Want ski school."

Tough! I will only see Jean-Lou twice more: this afternoon then tonight, then that's it. Mindfulness is all well and good, but my heart will be brim-full of pain when I'm on the way to the airport tomorrow.

"I won't go!" Claude declares.

Me neither, I think as my chest tightens painfully.

I pull Claude into a cuddle.

WE'RE ALL GLUM as we clomp our way down to the pistes through thick snow flurries. The humdrum rain, landscape and food of Lancashire are going to be a come-down for all of us. But at least their hearts are not going to be ripped apart.

It's still so new with Jean-Lou, partly because we were friends first. This deliciousness between us is a bonus. A massive, yummy bonus. And he's not going to criticise me, be disappointed in me, or worst of all, disapprove of me. He sees me for who I am and likes me anyway.

The worst part, though, is that I'm about to leave him with her, his monstrous mother.

Dominique, who's just clicked into her skis at the edge of the piste, glances over her shoulder at me standing by the ski racks, checking I'm there.

Not long after she disappears into the cloudy snow, Jean-Lou's shape emerges.

"Hey, cheer up, Nirvana! This is a special afternoon."

I'm shy with him in the daylight, even with the semi-light the falling snow allows.

"It is?"

He nods. "And you could never guess."

So, not our igloo? That's for tonight then. I beam, loving how he's turning what could be so miserable into something exciting.

I may be leaving soon, but not yet.

We set off even faster than usual towards the forest path, the opposite way to our new igloo.

As soon as we round the first corner, we stop simultaneously. Again, I'm shy, but he pulls me to him, and the feel and smell of him is familiar now. He stoops, and I twine my arms around his neck. With Jean-Lou, every kiss is important. He focuses entirely on me, always saying something. Today, it's, *Amazing to see you! Just you wait!*

TWENTY

A NOISE FILTERS THROUGH our kiss.
Yapping. And now howling!

"Wolves?"

He laughs. "Husky dogs!" His eyes sparkle. "Come and see!"

He tugs at my hand to hurry me on.

The second we turn the next corner, where the track opens out as it bends around the wedge of wood, I see it, my surprise: a sled and a whole *pack* of huskies!

Hoh! I catch my breath.

"This is my friend's team," he tells me. "I help him train them."

Hardly able to take this in, I shake my head.

"It's so we can reach the top of the mountain, and in time," he says.

Smiling, shaking my head, I bite my bottom lip. He's done all this for me?

He introduces me to his friend, Marc. I try to focus on him, this one friend of his, but find myself distracted by the dogs.

Five huskies.

One sheep dog.

All of them raring to go.

"*Trop d' énergie,*" Marc explains.

127

He introduces me to each of them, but they're distracted too, straining to be off. Except the sheep dog, Samson, one of the lead dogs. He stops, quietens, allows me to stroke his ears. I squat down to run my hand over his strong shoulders, snow ultra-white on his black coat, I know where he gets his name. He reminds me how much I've been missing Rova.

"Ready to go?" Marc asks me.

My pulse races as I straighten up. I glance at Jean-Lou in excitement.

"S'okay," he says, smiling. "I've done this so many times."

Which explains his strength.

"I'll meet you back here in a couple of hours," Marc says. He gestures to the upright sled as if to say, *It's all yours*, and off down a path to the right.

Jean-Lou tells me to step onto the wooden base at the back.

Feeling my weight, the dogs up their yowling.

"Hey! Don't leave me!" I yell to him in English.

What if they set off with me on my own? Much as I love dogs, I can't control six of them!

I crane around. He's checking the lead dogs' harnesses before climbing on, right behind me, reaching around me to hold on to the bar himself.

"Ready?" he asks, his breath warm near my ear.

Heart thumping, I nod.

"*Allez*, Samson, Miska!" he tells the two lead dogs.

We're off, careering around the rest of the corner.

"Lean left!" he says in my ear, as we counterbalance the bend.

Fast and wild, no time for thinking, the dogs surge ahead, spraying up snow that I have to blink away.

The path straightens out; the ride's smoother, calmer. You can only be in the instant on a ride like this: your senses race to keep up with

flashes of

white

beige, greys of the huskies

Samson's black patches stark against the snow

marigold sun

winking through fir trees

whirr of our rails cutting

snow

crisp, piny smell

cold ever icier on my cheeks.

Having worked off their giddiness, the pack quietens, steadies. We're all just enjoying the ride, gliding over the snow, trees on either side of us, watching us pass. I relax, trusting in the team and Jean-Lou, who's clamped to my back.

There's a buzzing, clanking, and I tip my head back, watching a chair lift pass overhead.

"Straight on!" Jean-Lou commands the team as a left fork cuts off, sharp and steep, back down to the ski station.

The dogs bark their understanding and career on, on and up, curving gently to the right, around Bear Mountain.

Soon, we start to level out. The team picks up speed again on a straight, flat stretch.

The snatches of white and green, the sharp of the air, pluck at my breath.

As the dogs turn right again, beginning to round the back of the mountain, they slow as the track steepens again. We ripple over a cattle grid.

Suddenly it's lighter ahead. The path opens out, and a bank of thick snow falls away to our right, running into a massive pine forest. Ahead is a tiny hamlet of chalets we swoosh between.

Picked out by the sun, spangles of snow twinkle at us as we flash past. The higher we go, the clearer it's becoming, till, over the dogs' bounding backs, I finally see it—

La Pointe du Mont!

I've seen it only in silhouette up till now—on Christmas Eve. The track hugs close to it, and soon the dogs are turning left to follow it to its peak. Up there is bright with sun. We *can* actually get above the clouds! It's the view I've waited for all week! If we're late back, I don't care. Nothing will stop us now.

Everything's slowing. The route's at its steepest, no longer 'groomed' by the piste basher, and the dogs are flagging with our combined weight. Higher than I've ever been, the air's sterile in its purity and beyond freezing on my face.

By now, we're around the back of this highest mountain, in its shadows but still with the promise of sun at its summit. The dogs are labouring to scramble over the deeper snow, whipped into drifts.

"Brace!" Jean-Lou booms in my ear.

We jolt back, forward as the dogs stop.

No more track.

We step off, shaking the tension out of our hands and arms. I help to give out biscuits from Jean-Lou's backpack.

"*Bravo!*" I tell each dog by name as I offer him or her a handful of biscuits and stroke between their ears.

Jean-Lou's now squinting up at the golden summit of La Pointe du Mont. "We have to walk from here."

"The dogs?"

"Look," he says and points. All six have settled down to rest, noses to tails.

"Stay!" he tells them, in his leader-of-the-pack voice.

Hand in hand, we start towards a steep slope and the peak.

He keeps tight hold of me all the way. Silent, we focus on digging our toes into the deep snow and levering ourselves out of each step, time after laborious time.

Breathing hard, I'm driven on by the brightness above, the hope of the view from the peak. Three times, I think we're at the top, but each time, there's a little more... until there isn't, and the ground starts to level. The cairn comes into sight, and I fix my gaze on the teetering tower of loose stones.

At the summit marker, I lean forward, hands on my thighs to recover my breath.

The sun warm on my shoulders, I straighten up. Jean-Lou puts his arm around my waist as together, we revolve slowly around the whole 360-degree panorama, large and live before us instead of in miniature on his relief map.

At last, I see it all.

As we turn, Jean-Lou names the mountain ranges, often with Dents in their name because of their toothy outlines. We can even glimpse the croissant of Lac Leman, Lake Geneva, near where he goes to collège.

"And that," he says, as we're almost back to the beginning, "is Mont Blanc."

Finally.

The highest mountain in Europe. Its spiky, rising peaks are crowned by a jagged, asymmetrical pyramid. Beautiful but foreboding.

I can finally see where I've spent a week of my life, and it's so much more than I imagined.

I turn to Jean-Lou. He's looking at me rather than the view.

"The sun's set it on fire!" he says, rippling his fingers over my hair.

"*Now* I understand why you love living here," I tell him.

Their drama, the extremeness of them, but also that from here, you can see so far, you can work out how things fit together.

"I love this world!" I shout with all my might.

Jean-Lou beams a huge smile and bends to kiss me.

You're as beautiful as all this, his kiss tells me.

You too, I tell him back.

I turn to take in the Alpine chain once more, groping in my pocket for my phone to capture this spectacle. I'm so gutted I can't send it to Grandad—I can hardly ask him not to mention it in front of Mum. But I *can* send it to Sab.

"Oh no!" I tell Jean-Lou after a minute. "I've forgotten my phone." It's still charging on my desk.

He hands me his.

Once I've taken the best panorama I can, I close his email account to open mine and bring up Sab's email address. I don't know her number by heart, but I want to send this to her right now, from right here.

In the Subject line above the image, I type:

Finally, mountains in the sun! They don't hide away; why should you and me?

I hand the phone back to him and sigh. "Sab and me... how can we stand proud and open, just as we are, like the mountains, without anything stopping us doing what we want?"

I really don't want to carry on, this having to hide the things that mean the most to me, including Jean-Lou.

He blows out his lips. "The biggest question of all. Back to freedom. Some of it's easier when we are adults, but..."

He shrugs at the impossibility of being totally free.

"You *are* like these mountains, though, Nirvana—strong."

Half-teasing, he wraps his fingers around my right bicep, which, thanks to woodwork, *is* pretty firm. But inside, I don't feel strong at all at the thought of going home.

"I have to send the application for my apprenticeship tomorrow. But Mum's still dead set against it."

"That's why you need an ally, like I have Papa. And now you have me."

My heart leaps. "I do?"

"Of course!" He sounds amazed I could think otherwise.

So, we're not just a sweet interlude, a Christmas diversion? Because we've not yet said one word about what happens once I've left.

"You have me too, Jean-Lou. But how are we ever going to see each other again after today?" My voice cracks. "How *can* we when my parents don't even know you exist?"

He loops his arms around my waist. "About that, Nirvana…"

He tells me his plan, and although our future sounds far from easy, far from certain, he wants it, is prepared to stick his neck out, to try. Maybe, together, we might just find a way to keep this—whatever it is between us—going.

I smile up at him, and we kiss.

When we pull apart, the light's fading fast. The sun's not going to reappear from behind this thick bank of clouds. Not today. We need to start our descent.

Snow starts to fall almost as soon as we leave the summit, huge flakes tumbling over themselves thicker than I've yet seen, almost angrily, from a sky that's become purple and bruised.

But I can't stop smiling. What Jean-Lou's just told me, his idea for how we can continue to see each other, proves we're strong too. And if we're strong, I'm strong.

"The dogs—won't they be cold?" I ask as we scramble back down the slope more or less in the tracks we made on the way up.

He gives me a wry smile. Of course, they're made for this climate. But it's the border collie I'm worried about. Samson hasn't the same coat as the rest of them.

I needn't have worried. Once we're over the ridge, from above, I spot him curled into Miska. A bit like us last night!

As we get nearer, one of them clocks us coming and alerts the others. Back on their paws, they set up a barking, this time in greeting.

We greet them back, telling them what good dogs they are. I ask if they've had a good nap, as if they're really going to answer me.

Down here, it's sombre with thick snow wiping out dusk and throwing us into night. At least the dogs can see, close to their terrain. We set off, retracing our tracks, faster than we came, seeing little but the two rear dogs and flakes slanting past us.

We emerge from the shadows of la Pointe du Mont, and soon we're around the front of Bear Mountain; lights from the village appear, but so subdued.

The dogs know they're on the homerun now. Quietly, steadily, smoothly, they're returning us to the wide corner we started from.

Marc's waiting there with his van and trailer.

I could, should, bomb down the track back to the village, thinking up some excuse for being late. But I don't want to miss a moment of this.

I say my thank-yous and goodbyes to the dogs, Samson in particular, while Jean-Lou and Marc speak to each other and unleash the dogs, who leap into their trailer, where bowls of food are ready for them.

"Time to get back," Jean-Lou says softly.

TWENTY-ONE

I F MY HEART's beating faster as I climb the steps to the chalet, it's not because I'm worried about the reaction to my being forty-five minutes late. I've got an excuse for that. It's the thought of eleven-thirty, at the entrance to Toblerone Wood, our early New Year's party and all the hours we'll have before morning. Nothing else matters apart from his plan, which will cause more than raised eyebrows but has to happen. It *will* happen, tomorrow morning.

It's chaos inside: ski clothes hang all over the hall when usually we leave them in the drying room in the garage; our ski boots are all bagged up. They're packing already. My heart lurches. Can't we pretend it's not happening? That we're not leaving tomorrow? Just for a little longer.

Dominique appears in their bedroom doorway, arms full of folded clothes.

"Ah, do not take your coat off, Nirvan-ah, I want you to take your skis and boots back to the hire shop."

I sigh. "Can't I do it in the morning?"

Claude belts out of his room and butts the top of his head into my stomach.

"Hey, Poodle, s'up?"

"He still does not want to go home," Dominique says over his head.

I stroke his back, knowing how he feels. A rare sob ripples down him.

137

When Dominique disappears, I crouch down to look at him properly.

"What if we go sledging in the morning, just you and me, eh? Unlike skiing, I'm actually good at that," I add, trying to make him laugh.

"But we won't be here tomorrow," he says, between more judders. "We're leaving now!"

"Ten minutes!" Dominique calls from their bedroom.

I straighten up, blood boiling.

"I'll see about that," I tell him.

I march into their room. Only Dominique's there, her back to me as she leans over a suitcase on the bed.

"When was anyone going to tell me?"

She stops for a second. "*Desolée, chou-chou*. I thought your mother already had."

"We can't leave today!"

I mean it. Nothing will stop me seeing Jean-Lou tonight. It would be the end of my world, literally.

"We must," Dominique says, half-turning to me. "Such heavy snow is forecast tonight, we will not get to the airport tomorrow. I have had to book a hotel in Geneva for tonight."

I shake my head. "No, that's ridiculous. The flight's not till five p.m. They're so used to snow here, they'll plough it no problem. Claude and I want a last night. We want to sledge together first thing in the morning. Cancel the hotel, Dominique, please."

She shakes her head. "You saw how much snow is on the road already. The *meteo* forecasts as much as two metres by morning. The ploughs have to focus on the main roads, not the minor ones over cols."

My blood's icy now. I know that tone. Tears burn at the back of my eyes.

I stalk out to find Mum. She's in the lounge, kneeling on the floor to cram toys and other stuff into a bag.

"Mum, surely we can still leave tomorrow? They never get snowed in up here."

"I honestly don't think we have a choice, love," she says. "We don't want to go early either."

Dominique comes in behind me and puts a hand on my shoulder. "Even I cannot control the snow, Nirvan-ah. I've had to do your packing for you since you were late back. Take your ski gear back now, please."

At a loss, I stride to the window and look out into the heavy flakes towards our igloo.

I won't go. I *can't* miss this last night with Jean-Lou. Because we haven't yet needed to exchange phone numbers, I can't even let him know I can't come. I picture him waiting at the start of Toblerone Wood.

Waiting and

waiting

and waiting.

Wondering if maybe I didn't *want* to come, if I've got cold feet about us. If he was just a diversion for me.

Before I give myself away with hot tears I can't explain, I bomb out of the room, shove my feet back into my snow boots and run down the steps to the garage.

Juggling boots and skis, balancing the helmet on my head, I get stuck in a drift up to my thighs as I struggle across the shortcut.

"Come on!" I moan as I haul one leg out. I've got to get to Jean-Lou.

The ski hire shop's already closed, thank God. I dump the whole friggin' lot in its porch and leg it as best as I can towards the resto.

To Jean-Lou.

I could just hide out with him. We could make for our igloo. No one would find us there.

Even as I think it, I know it won't work. My family couldn't leave, search parties would be called. No possible future for us then.

But if I can only tell him what's happening, we can work on a Plan B. We can sort it, together. And I can at least give him my phone number.

The road is thickly covered. I run up the path to the resto. It's locked! It's still early—the big feast won't start till much later—so I dart around to the side of the building. A light's on upstairs, in their apartment. Jean-Lou's up there, but I can't reach him. There's a little balcony. With all my mental might, I will him outside.

A car horn beeps.

"What on earth are you doing all the way across here, Nirvan-ah?" Dominique's voice screeches through the snow. "You have been ages. Get in!"

"No!" I yell before the wind can whip my words away. "I...I...I haven't finished..."

"You have." As certain as ever. "I have checked your room. Now, in the car, before we are stranded here."

I step right back, looking up at the flat. If Jean-Lou appears, I won't care if they see me with him.

I just need to explain, so he knows I'd never change my mind about him.

To swap contact details.

To say *au revoir*.

140

TWENTY-TWO

DOMINIQUE ACTUALLY GETS out of the car. "You are behaving ridiculously, Nirvan-ah!" She stomps over, grabs my arm and bundles me into the back.

My parents, the weather, fate... all the powers that are, have conspired against us.

I'll never see Jean-Louis again runs through my head on repeat. *I'll never see him again. Never see him again.* How can I when I don't even have his phone number? What will he think when I don't show up?

That *I'm* rejecting him now?

I feel genuinely nauseous—that feeling when something horrible's happened and there's not a thing to be done about it. Like Nana's death. That utter powerlessness. Jean-Lou's alive, so alive, but dead to me if we will never see each other again.

I can see no way now for Mum and Dominique to meet him. His plan was to deliver our breakfast pastries to us in the morning, for me to introduce him, who his dad is, for him to explain how we'd met on the pistes, which isn't even a lie. For us both to tell them how we want him to come to Lancashire at half-term for the sake of our French and English. He'd win them over, I know he would.

But now...

I cry as rarely as Claude, but the tears trickling down to my chin are for Jean-Lou. He'll be wishing the time on, willing it to be eleven-thirty as he downloads our songs, packs baguette and cheeses, fizzy drinks.

Betrayal is what it feels like. Cruelty. Even though it's the last thing I'd ever do to him.

Not a word is spoken all the way down the mountain. We're all lost in our separate misery.

HEAVY SNOW BECOMES heavy rain once we reach the valley, but instead of more crying, I shrivel up, dry up, shut down. On our way into Geneva, its glistening lake has been replaced by a rat-grey fog. Jean-Lou and mountain life in full colour this afternoon has been reduced to black and white.

I look across at Claude, flashes of his little face fixed in unhappiness every time we go under a streetlight. He'll be fine when we get home, though, once he sees Rova and Grandad. But not even they will ease this suffocating feeling of losing Jean-Lou. It's like homesickness that'll never end.

I give myself up to numb despair.

AT ELEVEN-THIRTY, WITH Claude thrashing around in the single bed next to me, the pain kicks in again. So clearly can I see Jean-Lou looking out for me from the wood. I should be there with him, in our igloo. Our perfect igloo we had only one night in. We had less than twenty-four hours for kissing!

Midnight strikes. He'll wait, I know he will. Will he go back down into the village or to our igloo in case I thought we were meeting there?

Twelve-thirty... He'll know now I'm not coming. What a slap in his face, a kick in his teeth after the husky ride, our mountaintop view, our extraordinary kisses last night, to have left without a word. If his mother finds out, she will rub his face in it. He knows how I feel, but that woman's more than capable of making it far, far worse for him.

I glance across at Claude, finally, unhappily asleep. My little brother and me are stuck in this soulless hotel room when we should be preparing for one last morning of sledging.

When I should be with Jean-Lou in our lovingly made igloo.

My heart's in actually physical pain that I'm in the wrong place.

I JOLT AWAKE. The streetlit room blasts it into my brain that this is *not* the blissful black of our igloo or even the chalet. My heart nosedives.

It's 1.27 a.m., my tracker tells me.

Then I realise! I sit bolt upright. Of course!

I make a grab for my phone off the bedside table. It scutters off the plastic surface onto the wooden floor. Claude twitches at the clatter. Sneaking out of bed, I retrieve it from under the bed and, frantic, hold down the button on the side. I'd turned off my phone, unable to cope with messages from Sab, Grandad, anyone.

Except Jean-Lou, of course! I hold my breath as the screen lights up.

Yes! It's charged. I jab in my code. Okay. Click on email. My heartbeat's a hammer in my ears as the circles whirl on my screen. Thank God I left my phone behind yesterday and had to use Jean-Lou's at the summit. There was a reason for it: we're not star-crossed like Romeo and Juliet, after all!

I think, I hope, I *pray* I left my email account open. Surely, if he wants to find me, he'll think of that?

I hold my breath as I look for new emails, in bold.

But no. Not a single one.

My heart slows again.

Come on, Jean-Lou, I will him. *Think!*

I clamber back into bed, gazing at my phone like it's the most gripping film ever.

Except this is no film. It's my life.

PART II:
1 JANUARY

ONE

AS WE DRIVE home from Manchester airport, Lancashire is drab and brown under torrents of rain, its hills pathetic after the drama of the Alps. But my mind—it's full of yesterday's unbelievable husky ride with Jean-Lou to the glorious mountaintop view.

Not because I'm torturing myself but because, when I checked my phone on waking in Geneva, this:

> *j.jaboulay 1:43 a.m.*
>
> *Chère Nirvana*
>
> *I waited for half an hour at our place; checked the village, the woods and our igloo. When you didn't come by one a.m., I thought you must have had to leave early with your family because of the snow. I'm sorry not to have had the opportunity to meet them.*
>
> *I hope it's all right that I used your email address from your account you left open? I realised you didn't have any way to contact me. So here is my email address, my WhatsApp name and my phone number.*

Happy New Year, Nirvana—shall we reschedule our party?

In hope,
Jean-Lou

My fingers replied instantly, my heart dictating.

He waited for hours in the freezing cold! For me!

I heard the teeny signs of uncertainty in his questions and certain phrases, but at the same time, my Jean-Lou isn't afraid to put his heart on the line—'in hope', he said. And that's because he's sure of mine. What we have *is* extraordinary.

Next, I WhatsApped him. And when I finally escaped my family at Geneva airport, I phoned him. It was strange at first, only having our voices, but when I get home, we'll find private times to FaceTime and I'll actually be able to see him too!

Best of all, we came up with a Plan B.

Even though we don't have the same half-term in February, he could come here for a long weekend.

So, first my parents have to know about him.

In some form.

There it gets tricky. Our best thought so far is, we stick with our true story that we met on the pistes. Because Mum and Dominique actually know who his dad is, have even talked to him, however briefly, Jean-Lou will ask him to email them to suggest language exchange visits, though both of us know there's no way I can go and stay there with Ghislaine. It's horribly disturbing to think that so far, the only person who has any idea about us is *her*.

What I can easily picture, though, is Jean-Lou here, meeting Rova, playing with Claude—he'll get the measure of him and be honest but kind with him at the same time. Just the thought of it makes me glow inside.

"*Les ado!*" Dominique says, shaking her head at me in the rear-view mirror. "One minute, you refuse to leave the Alps, and now you are happy to be back."

That wipes the smile off my face somewhat. My body longs for nothing more than to be with my heart and head in the Alps, but at least being in touch with Jean-Lou all the time will make home bearable. And I'm going to show them all in my mocks, so Mum and Dominique will know I'm going to be an apprentice not because I'm no good at anything else but because it's what I really want to do.

As we get nearer home, my mind *has* to come back here. Yeah, that's a question for Montaigne—mindfulness is all well and good when your present is something wonderful, like being with Jean-Lou. But what about when it's somewhere you'd rather *not* be?

We pass the turning to the Pendle Grove. My neglected oak boards needle my mind. At the moment, they're stored safely under tarpaulin in the heart of the woods, but now I must get them inside before the very wettest months. And how am I ever going to get the miner's table constructed by the end of January when I've missed two weeks' work on them, when mocks loom like a battleline against me, and it's going to rain constantly? I can't really expect Sab to have found somewhere indoors for them when I asked around at the bowling green and Brownie HQ and couldn't even come up with a little hut.

ONCE WE TURN onto Castle View, I spot Grandad's car outside our house, meaning he's brought Rova home! We open the front door and everything happens at once! While the four of us are all squashed in the hallway, Rova pushes past everyone else, all the cases, and makes straight for me. She must have really missed me! Feeling a bit of a traitor that I've been so caught up in Jean-Lou, I drop to the floor, wrapping my arms around her.

"Hello, my sweetest one," I murmur into her neck.

And suddenly I am home after all. At least in the sense of being with my oldest friend.

I hold onto her until she wants to go. She runs, actually runs, between me and Claude at either end of the hall. I clap her each time she comes back to me. I've not seen her this energetic for months!

Finally, she exhausts herself and slinks off to collapse in the living room.

I rush after her to find Grandad.

He's on the settee, Claude on the rug, already chatting nineteen to the dozen to him about skiing.

"Hey, my Sunshine," Grandad says, his arm tightening around me as I sink down next to him. "What did you enjoy most about the Alps, love? Let someone else get a word in for a moment, Sonny Jim," he tells Claude, who's still wittering on.

"Who's Sunny Jim?" Claude asks, looking around the room as if some other chatterbox is there.

Grandad shakes his head at me over Claude, but I've a lump in my throat because I can't tell him all the things I'd love to. I can't show him that amazing panorama I took only yesterday or tell him about igloos, huskies and even Jean-Lou. Even though he'd totally get their attractions over ski lessons, I can't put him in the position of having to keep secrets from Mum too.

"How's your Christmas been, Grandad?" I ask instead.

"You've not been worrying about me and Rova, have you, Niv? It really did work out for the best. And you look like you've been having the holiday of a lifetime."

Relieved, I smile at him. "I really have!"

Mum comes in with a tray of brews and biscuits, and the conversation pings back to parallel turns, moguls, jumps and slaloms with Claude trying to demonstrate on the rug.

I crawl across to Rova, who's not remotely interested in skiing either. Thumping her tail on the carpet, she struggles to sitting, and I hide my head in her mane again, starting to feel overwhelmed.

Today is the deadline for my apprenticeship application to the CITB, and Mum still hasn't said anything more about it. Mocks, a place to build my miner's table—those are for tomorrow.

And all this without Jean-Lou.

I breathe out a massive sigh. Rova licks my nose, trying to convince me it'll be all right.

I take a selfie of me and her.

My other best friend, Rova I add as a caption as I WhatsApp it to Jean-Lou, even while everyone else is there.

151

Very beautiful! He messages back right away.

Hey! You said the same about me! I joke.

At once, I feel less cut off and trapped, knowing we can be in touch anytime, anywhere, even right under my family's noses. But that's another thing against the odds I've got to pull off, and soon: get over the sky-high hurdle of telling my parents about him and convince them it's a good idea that he comes over, never mind stopping his mother standing in our way. I can only leave that to Jean-Lou and trust his lovely dad will be on our side.

Now, though, I've got to get on with the most urgent item on my list of life-changing tasks—one that Jean-Lou is convinced I'm strong enough to pull off, even on my own.

So, I tear myself away from Rova, say goodbye to Grandad and take my bag upstairs.

TWO

I FIRE UP MY laptop; click on the Documents folder and choose *Application form*.

Thank goodness I actually thought ahead for once and filled this in some weeks ago. If only Mum was sitting next to me, doing this last check.

I imagine marching downstairs and just telling her what I'm about to do, asking her one last time if she'll help. If she'll back my application because it's not so much about the form but what it means for my future. I *know* what her answer would be, though, and that even asking would make it harder for when I ever dare introduce the existence of Jean-Lou.

Nope, I'm gonna have to keep on hiding this away for now. But as Jean-Lou said to me not much more than twenty-four hours ago, I have him as my ally now, and his voice in my head reminds me, *If your self is to work with wood, Nirvana, you must.*

As the application form opens in front of me, it actually feels exactly the right thing to be doing New Year's Day. New year, new Niv, and best of all, *I'm* the one choosing the direction.

It's all straightforward personal info until I get to—

English and Maths results/expected result:

153

I sigh. Six weeks ago, when I intended to stick to the revision timetable Dominique drew up for me, I was hoping for even better than the numbers I put in. But now...

Stupid friggin' exams! I sit up tall. I was doing other things in December, creating actual objects, things for my family: Christmas presents, a table, for goodness' sake!

I know what I'm doing, I want to write instead of the numbers. *My grandad's given me all this knowledge and understanding and love of trees. I've spent a year learning the basics of woodwork. I'm longing to build.*

But there's no space for words, only single figures.

I gaze at the numbers that seemed attainable not that long ago.

5 for Maths; 5 for English.

My finger hovers over the downward arrow.

But I've only lost focus a bit. Even if I don't quite make it in the mocks, I will in the end. Won't I?

I move my finger and move on.

Chosen career path:

Now my heart bounds. This is *me* choosing this! The first important choice I've ever been able to take. A path, that begins right now and weaves to my future.

Apprenticeship in Joinery

154

Only the last question is still unanswered—one I was going to discuss with Mum.

> Would you be willing to stay away from home
> if necessary?

I hesitate. But only for a second.

YES, I tap in.

Once they've got my registration, I know what happens next better than I know my mocks timetable—not that that's saying much!

Their system tries to match you with employer vacancies. These can come up any time from the start of the new year, so I've got to be ready.

If you get a match, you get an email. You take it from there. You submit your CV and cover letter straightaway. Then, *if* you're good enough, the individual company requests your portfolio by their own deadline.

My covering letter's good to go. My portfolio photos of Querky are up to date as far as I've got, and my blueprint of the miner's table is ready. It's urgent now I get on with actually building it.

If the CITB finds me a match, I could be striding towards my dream before the end of January!

Pulse pittering, I press 'send'.

I have done it! I WhatsApp to Jean-Lou. **Sent off my application! Xxxxxxx**

Bravo, Nirvana! he writes back at once. *Your journey begins!*

I breathe out all my tension. Having actually done what I've built up to for so long, it feels right, no niggles, no doubts.

Once I've sent Jean-Lou a smiley face, I throw my phone onto the bed and force my eyes to the mocks timetable stuck on my desk. Thank God we get Monday as a study day. Then first off, on Tuesday morning, as I knew, is Eng Lit. At least I've finished the set novel. Now there's just the little problem of the poetry. Worse, far worse, is the afternoon. Chemistry. Just the word is enough to strike fear into me.

Time to call in my ally at home.

THREE

THE NEXT MORNING, Sab's sharp eyes scrutinise my face as I sit on my bed, leaning against the wall. I gaze at the multicoloured hot-air balloons sailing all over her hijab, one of her vast range of head coverings I've not seen before. The balloons speak of freedom and adventure and make me smile as I imagine gently, silently, gliding over the whole chain of the Alps I saw just the day before yesterday. With Jean-Lou, of course.

"It's as I suspected, Niv," Sab announces, leaning back on my desk chair. "You've got it bad."

I beam, entirely happy with her diagnosis.

"But how could you possibly have known what was happening that first night, way before I did?"

She shakes her head, despairing of me. "No one would offer to go out in the freezing cold all the time unless he was also harbouring some hope."

I grin at the thought: Jean-Lou said he felt it right from the start! "But that doesn't explain how you knew I liked him back."

"Obvs." Her eyebrows show her surprise that I even need to ask. "You were playing it down to protect yourself against disappointment."

I blow out my lips in recognition. What film did she get that from?

157

"But no need to worry," she says, sitting forward to inspect me again, like some specimen. "That glow, Niv, it's all the dopamine and serotonin in your system."

I scowl at what's between me and Jean-Lou being reduced to hormone-related symptoms. "You been revising biology?"

"It'll work its way out," Sab goes on, in full doctor mode, "now you're no longer together."

That stabs at my heart.

"Only temporarily," I say. "We're gonna keep this going, Sab, obviously. He's coming to stay at Feb half-term."

She nearly falls off her chair!

"And your parents are cool with that?"

I lean back against the wall. "No, but they will be."

"So they've met him?"

I'm starting to feel stupid now. "They've met his dad."

I explain where he lives, then I swivel around to rest back on my headboard, as if I've proved myself. She's gone quiet, pondering.

Finally, she gives me one of her sharp looks. I brace myself for more of her straight-talking. "You're gonna prolong the pain. It must have been amazingly romantic, Niv. But it was a holiday fling."

My whole body goes hot and rigid at the ridiculous phrase while I try to work out how to convince her how totally wrong she is.

"Enjoy it for what it was, Niv," she says, her tone softening. "Look at Romeo and Juliet. They only had one obstacle—their families. You two've got a whole *heap* of odds against you."

"No, no, we haven't!" I say, fierce now. "Just geography, that's all."

She gives me one of those *Really?* looks that are more infuriating than any words. We both know, my family might not be at war with Jean-Lou's, but no way are they gonna support us. I especially can't tell Sab about Ghislaine. That really would fuel her argument.

"We won't let anything or anyone stand in our way," I tell her, slow and clear, even though we don't yet have a Plan C if our Plan B doesn't work.

"I know you think that now," she starts again. "But you really are in a right Romeo and Juliet sit, Niv. Falling fast, forbidden love, separation 'n' all that. And you know it don't end well for Juliet."

I sigh in frustration.

"We're so not them, Sab! We're not star-crossed for a start!" Quite the opposite when I think of that shooting star that triggered our first kiss. "And way more importantly, we know each other loads better than Romeo and Juliet did. By the first time we kissed, *five days* after we met, I knew him better than anyone."

Instantly, I feel guilty, saying this to my bestie. But why shouldn't I be as straight with her as she is with me?

"What, in a week?"

"Yes, in a week!" I can't properly explain how we compressed months into days. "I can talk to him about anything. Everything."

"Yeah, well, you can talk to me about everything, too, Niv."

Guilt prickles again, that I ended up telling Jean-Lou about my apprenticeship before her.

After another moment, she shrugs. "I'm sure it could have turned into...something, Niv. But..."

While she spreads her hands to express what she sees as our minuscule odds, the jagged part of my heart, sore from being ripped away from Jean-Lou without even saying *au revoir,* stings like hell at the prospect of never seeing him again. It'd be grief; proper, full-on grief.

I huff and shake my head. I really need Sab to understand this.

"Me and Jean-Louis, we already *are* something. So, we *have* to carry on being. It's not just a...fancying thing." We're both so off-beat in our different ways, it's incredible we fit so beautifully with each other.

"Finding a lad was the last thing on my mind," I go on. "But now it's happened, we can't just throw it away. I'll *never* find someone who it works with in *every* way, like with him. It feels...right, for both of us."

She twists her mouth like maybe I've edged her off her sceptical perch, or at least silenced her for a bit.

Digging the chem books out of her handbag, she starts slowly turning the pages, and I force myself to focus, to copy down formulae onto index cards. Sab's got a really good memory, though, when she bothers to read the material, whereas I have to write it out, check it back, correct it. We test each other at the end of each chapter, and by lunchtime, we've got some knowledge in our brains. I just don't understand what it means!

When Mum shouts up with a ten-minute lunch warning, Sab starts to pack her stuff away and we both stand.

"Sorry for giving you a hard time, Niv, about your Jean-Louis." She sniffs, looks down then gives me a half-smile. "Cruel to be kind—I don't want to see you all cut up if something *does* get in your way."

My heart expands. I know her refusal to tell me what I want to hear *is* about caring.

"You and I have a pretty good record at not letting things stand in our way, don't we?"

"Yeah," she agrees, "we do. And I might just have made some progress on the building location for that Alpine table you showed me."

I catch my breath. "Really? What? Where? Why didn't you tell me before?"

She mock sways back at my barrage of questions then taps the side of her nose.

"It's your mocks this week, Nirvan-ah!"

"You're the best," I tell her. Even though it'll drive me mad waiting to find out what she's come up with for my boards, I know she's right to make me focus.

But what if she's also right to prepare me for the worst with Jean-Lou? I ponder on this as I make my way slowly towards the kitchen. My grand claim that nothing will stop us seeing each other again is all well and good, but what if my parents do flatly refuse? If he'd met them, as we planned, they'd have taken to him—how could they not! But can I really expect them to agree to a lad they've never met coming to stay?

Dominique's made a roast chicken dinner and nothing, bar nothing, puts me off my food. But I escape the second I can get away with it, saying I need some fresh air. Grabbing my phone and Parka, I stride out into the rain.

As soon as I'm out of the front garden, I tap Jean-Lou's number.

FOUR

"Nirvana, *salut!*" His voice is warm with pleasure, instantly easing my doubts.

"Hi! Where are you, Jean-Lou?"

"I'm in the forest—on my way back from our igloo. Just a sec."

He briefly switches to video and gives me a flash of our snowy Toblerone wood. The pull to be there with him is sharp, which is why we soon stopped using video to see each other.

"Do you go to our igloo every day?"

He pauses. "Yep. I'm spending a lot of time there."

Then I get why. His mother. I can hear it in the flatness of his voice, the shades of which I'm just getting to know. I should be there.

"And it's stopped snowing at last," he says brightly, changing the subject.

"It's rained here ever since I got back."

"You're not selling England to me very well!"

"You're coming to see me, not England, aren't you?"

"I'm coming to see you, Nirvana," he confirms.

I beam. "So, you've asked your dad, about coming in February?

I duck into the bus shelter at the end of Castle View.

"Yes. In fact…"

Then I get lost. It's harder to follow his French when I can't see his mouth.

"Slow down, Jean-Lou, please. In fact what?"

"In fact, I told him about you...us. But..."

I'm dying to know how he describes 'us' but let him continue.

"He already knew, he says."

"What? How did he know? From her...your mother?"

A pause.

"Jean-Lou?"

"No. He says..." I can hear the sheepishness in his voice. "He says I'm so much happier."

Laughing, I go all warm inside. "That's something like Sab said about me!" Though she knew before she ever even saw me!

We both go quiet, a bit shy.

"Anyway," Jean-Lou says after a moment. "Papa says yes, he is happy to write to your parents to suggest a language exchange, especially since he's met them and you and thinks you're a lovely family."

"Great! You'd better get working on your English then," I say in English.

"*Quoi*? What was that, Nirvana?" he says, lost.

"Not important. So even your mother agrees to you coming?"

He snorts. "We don't ask her." He pauses. "What if he writes an email very soon and you can forward it to your parents when you are ready?"

I nod eagerly, as if he can see me. "Yes, that will work. I can send it once my exams are finished."

I'm going to *have* to face Mum and Dominique then because we need to get flights booked before they're too dear, *plus* we both need a date to focus on. It'll help Jean-Lou with her, Ghislaine, if he has it to look forward to. As well as me, obviously.

"We will see each other next month!" I tell him.

"I know!" His tone's as excited as mine.

But a month's a loooooooong time when you're unhappy.

"What're you doing today?" he asks after a pause.

"I revised chemistry this morning, with Sab. Maths, this afternoon."

"I'd better let you get on with that, Nirvana," he says. "So...till tomorrow."

That makes me smile. He said that most of our days in Ouzon.

"Till tomorrow, Jean-Lou."

As I trudge home towards maths cramming, my doubts rear their heads again. Not about Jean-Lou. He feels as strongly as ever, I know he does. It's just the image of me forwarding an email from Jean-Lou's dad to my mum seems such a fantasy. Maybe if she and Dominique actually knew Jean-Lou existed. Maybe if I wasn't going to do an apprenticeship they're totally opposed to. Maybe if I wasn't going to bomb these mocks.

Not too late to make a difference, I tell myself as I open our front door. I've got to. My and Jean-Lou's future hinges on it.

FIVE

Today's all about *study*, I remind myself over my Weetabix the next morning.

Claude's finally started preschool. While Mum takes him, I manage to squeeze in a quick call with Jean-Lou from my bedroom, just as he gets to Thonon but before he goes into collège. He hasn't time to find a quiet spot, so I can't avoid snatches of animated French voices, some of them girls'. Jealousy stabs away at me as I imagine long, sleek, dark hair. Even though he sounds genuinely made up to have these extra few minutes together, eventually, he's going to meet someone local, isn't he? Someone who can be in his life all the time.

I sit up straighter on my desk chair. Jean-Lou doesn't want to meet someone else. He wants *me*, and I'm gonna keep it that way! I've got to do the very best possible in these mocks, then I can approach Mum about his visit.

Burying my phone under my pillow, I open *East of Eden* on my eReader, the set of revision note cards Dominique gave me back in November empty in front of me. Rivulets of rain streaming down my bedroom window catch my eye. The front door rattles, forcing my eyes back to my screen.

East of Eden's such a friggin' long novel, suited only to immortals, such as most others at Presdale Girls', supernatural beings with detailed notes on themes and character. This mortal's just going to swipe through the intro, looking for quotes she can wangle into any essay. Luckily, Steinbeck has lots to say about his own story. My eyes run over the sentences.

This one snags my attention. Oh God!

The greatest terror a child can have is that he is not loved. Rejection is the hell he fears.

That's Cal, of course, but it's Jean-Lou too. Living with *her* constant rejection, her taunting and mocking driving him to build an igloo to escape to. I could hear his unhappiness surfacing from time to time yesterday. She seems to be getting worse the older he gets, the less control she has over him.

Cal's making me think too much of Jean-Lou. I shove my eReader to one side. And anyway, there are some Frost poems I haven't read yet. I retrieve my phone from my bed and run downstairs.

"I'm gonna listen to poetry on BBC Bitesize while I get some air," I tell Mum, who's making some notes for one of her counselling clients at the kitchen table.

"In the rain?" she says, but she's used to my urges to 'tramp around outside', as she puts it.

NOT SURPRISINGLY, LISTENING to Frost's *Birches* propels my feet towards the Grove and my own lovely birches there. I've just turned down the quiet lane to the woods when Jean-Lou calls. He's just come out of philosophy and wants to tell me that they actually read one of Montaigne's essays, on friendship.

If philosophy was an option at my school, I'd be doing a whole lot better, I think as he tells me a bit about it.

"I've just arrived at the woods," I tell him, "to check on my boards."

"How are they, in the wet?"

"Can you stay on a little longer, so I can show you?"

I switch to 'view' and first of all show him the red sign at the edge of the trees.

DANGER, DEEP PITS

"Nirvana!" he exclaims. "Why are you going somewhere dangerous? What's this 'pits'?"

"Don't worry!" I tell him. "I know my way perfectly because Grandad brought me here with Rova from when I was three." Teaching me all the different leaf shapes.

I angle my phone towards the mossy depressions. "And these are the old pits."

"*Ah! Les fosses*," Jean-Lou tells me.

Avoiding the frequent dimples and ducking under dripping branches, I'm soon at my clearing.

"And there it is," I tell Jean-Lou, from the edge. "If I cannot be in our igloo, this is my happy place."

It feels strange after a two-week absence. So much has changed with me but nothing much with my clearing, save for a few final leaves added to the soggy, bronze carpet. I stride towards my bed of planks, safely stashed between two tall birches, and peel back the tarpaulin. I run my hand across the top, golden board and blow out a long breath.

"Look!" I show Jean-Lou. "All safe and dry!" And beautifully seasoned now.

I love how we're managing to wrap our lives together, despite the miles.

"Excellent! That's a lot of wood you've prepared, Nirvana. All from your grandad's oak?"

"Yep," I say, straightening up, though there is so much more of Querky still at Hackspace. "And Sab has an idea for where I can build it—after the mocks."

"She sounds such a good friend," he says.

A buzzer sounds, and suddenly he has to go, to science.

I pat my bed of boards. *Soon you're going to be transformed into a glorious table!*

Now I can visualise exactly what they're going to be, it feels so much closer, more possible than when I was last prepping them.

I'll be back for you! I promise them.

Have to be.

BACK AT MY desk, I manage to write down a few words from the three poems on my revision cards. By then it's lunchtime, so I'm going to have to count on one of those three coming up and wing it with *Romeo and Juliet*. This afternoon, Mum's got two past maths papers lined up for us to work through together, focusing on 'any problem areas'.

Mum tries and fails to hide her shock at how much help I need with the maths. I never struggled with it till Year 10. The content got harder, my new teacher was less clear, and I was less focused. If only I'd taken Mum up on her offers to help me months ago! I can finally ask the stupid questions I never dare ask in school, and it's so much better having something explained to you one-to-one and at your level. Actually, it's like someone's finally speaking my language when Ms. Bailey speaks some foreign one. But *too little too late* is the distinct feeling hanging in the air between us as Mum leaves to collect Claude.

Playing Labyrinth with him turns out to be a good way for him to tell me snippets about preschool. Sounds like his new friend Shazad is as full-on crazy as him. After tea, I go back over the chem formulae, but they make even less sense than yesterday. I have a sudden inspiration, though, since I found out this morning that Jean-Lou's still doing science as part of his *Bac Littérair*. Under the quilt, to muffle my voice, I ring him.

"Jean-Lou," I whisper, "can you help me understand chemistry in five minutes?"

"Not my favourite subject either, Nirvana, but I'll try," he whispers back, for some reason. "Which part?"

I pause, trying to pick out something specific. "Atoms? They're pretty important."

"Very!" he agrees. "Atoms make up elements, and that's what chemistry is all about—the way elements connect to create change."

"Okay, makes sense."

"And some atoms, such as hydrogen are like you and me—unstable on their own. So, they have to find each other."

"Mm," I smile under my quilt.

"They're then so entangled, they remain connected to each other even when separated by great distances."

"Incredible!" I murmur.

"Yep. And so much so, if something happens to one particle, it also happens to the other."

"That's us too," I whisper.

We have one of our happy silences before we finally agree we'd better get some sleep.

"Sleep well, Nirvana. À demains."

I drift into sleep, relaxed and happy.

SIX

"ALL RIGHT, NIV?" Sab's waiting for me at the traffic lights and, seeing my expression in the cold light of the impending chemistry mock, hands me a Double Decker. Chocolate's her usual breakfast, and it seems to work for me too.

Half an hour into the exam, there's nothing more I can do. Sadly, Jean-Lou's romantic take on chemistry I loved so much last night doesn't help one bit with these complicated questions. It leaves me with a torturous hour of watching all the girls in front of me scribble away with calculations and explanations of experiments.

On the piece the scrap paper we were each given for workings out, I re-sketch the blueprint for my miner's table. Now it's not having shelves, which saves me a lot of unnecessary time, I need to decide what to do with the upper half, the part above the table. I brainstorm a few ideas—

a mirror
a painting on the wood
a cork board to pin photos to...

Then I have it! I know, *just know*, it's the answer, and when I draw it onto my sketch, it looks complete.

It's Ms. Parekh herself who takes in the papers, and I feel a pang of guilt when I hand my disgrace of an exam script to her. As everyone starts scraping their chairs and the keanos make a beeline for each other to dissect the questions, this tightness forms inside me. I should never have been doing separate sciences in the first place, and anyway, what's chemistry got to offer wood manufacturing?

I don't go out for break—don't want to hear what everyone else thought of the paper. I stay at my desk and read the rest of the intro to *East of Eden*, but the references to Cal makes me worry about Jean-Lou again, and I can't even message him because Mum made me leave my phone at home.

When everyone else comes back in for a revision session, smelling of fresh air and smugness, I feel even more of a loser. Even though my apprenticeship doesn't require a science, I know deep down it matters. Ms. Parekh'll be disappointed in me. I'll be disappointed in myself. And disappointment will become disapproval when Mum and Dominique hear, especially as physics is going to be every bit as bad. My tummy churns.

SAB'S WAITING FOR me outside the exam hall. "Coming for some dinner?"

"I'll come, but I'm not eating," I say, feeling nauseous at the thought of the tuna sandwich Mum's made me.

"S'up?" she asks, as we make our way towards the canteen and she joins the queue. "Pining for Jean-Louis?"

I shake my head. "Chemistry was beyond a catastrophe."

172

When we find a table, Sab pushes her cardboard sleeve of fries across to me. "These are great when you're feeling that way."

I seriously doubt it but take a couple anyway to please her. And actually, they're delicious.

"We've only just started, Niv," she says. "Don't let one paper put you off."

My shoulders sag as a long sigh escapes me. "I've left it too late. For everything."

She shoves the chips towards me. "They're mocks, Niv, that's the point. You've still got time to pull yourself together for the real thing."

"That's the problem. I haven't."

Now I do what I should have done weeks ago if I hadn't been holding out to break it to Mum first. I tell her about my apprenticeship, the level fives I estimated myself in maths and English and how I need to send in school's official predictions as soon as they're done.

"Hm," she says before disappearing off for more chips.

"And, on top of all that," I tell her when she returns, "I've got to have my miner's table ready by the end of January."

She puts the carton of chips between us on the table. "What you need, Niv, is to start believing you can pull this off."

I sigh again. It'll need more than self-belief to be finished in time.

"Friday afternoon, when we've got the worst of the exams over," Sab says, "you'll have your wood inside, so you can start building over the weekend."

I shake my head in amazement. "I...I don't know how to thank you!"

"Tell me what happens at the end of *East of Eden*!" she says.

On the way to the exam hall, I give Sab a summary of Cal's journey and the main themes.

"You can defo ace this exam," she says, looking suitably impressed.

I gather myself up. This afternoon *will* make up for chem.

When I open the paper, I skip past the poetry section where the Frost question will be to get to the questions on Prose.

> 'A story about adults and the choices they make.' How far do you agree with this as a description of *East of Eden*?

Ms. Settle always says to make a plan to gather your thoughts. I don't need to gather mine. I can't usually find more than three paragraphs to say, yet I'm still writing forty-five minutes later, Ghislaine Jaboulay vivid in my mind. This'll rock the 'personal response' criterion, and I even back up what I say from the text. But I've spent way too much time on it and quickly move on to the *Romeo and Juliet* question.

> How far do you think the destiny of Romeo and Juliet's relationship was decided from the moment they met?

I set to, scribbling madly. *Not at all!!* If their families had just let them get on with it, they'd have been together happily as-long-as-ever-they-wanted!

Then I stop writing and start thinking about me and Jean-Lou. Ironically, we'd never have met but for Dominique's surprise ski trip. And but for him avoiding his mother and me cutting ski lessons, we'd not have intersected at our igloo either. Where it went wrong is Dominique deciding we had to leave for the airport a night early; otherwise, they'd have met Jean-Lou, loved him. So, what's really infuriatingly unfair is that just like for Romeo and Juliet, it's down to parents whether we can keep seeing each other or not.

A relationship doesn't have to end violently, I can't help thinking, *to end tragically.*

But I'm determined we'll have a happy ending, Jean-Lou and me.

"Five minutes!" the invigilator calls.

Nowhere near finished, I look down at my page in horror and scribble a conclusion that the prince is right when he concludes in the final lines of the play that the blame lies with the parents.

Sab's waiting for me again. This time, it's her who's not had a good one; it's clear at once from her droopy body language.

"At least with the poetry section, you get the poem in front of you. But did we ever even study that one?" she asks.

Noooo! I forgot the friggin' Frost! A third of the marks already lost.

"Which one was it?" I force myself to ask, half-hoping it's not one I knew.

Sab looks at me in disbelief.

"Here." She pushes her Mars bar my way. "You need this more than me."

At least luck is on my side when I get home. Mum's gone for Claude so I can retrieve my phone from the kitchen table and ring Jean-Lou.

"Nirvana!" he answers at once, like his phone's in his hand.

"Hi, Jean-Lou. Good time for you?"

"Just on the bus back from college, but most people have got off already. How were the exams?"

I sigh. "A catastrophe. Especially chemistry!"

"Really sorry it didn't go better," he commiserates.

"How was collège?"

Now he sighs. "Collège."

"How's the weather?" I ask, wanting to visualise his surroundings.

"Very strange. It's suddenly become warm. The snow's all melting."

I catch my breath. "Our igloo too?"

"I'll go to check later. But because it's deep in the woods and the blocks are very thick, it should still be frozen. If the weather goes cold again soon, it'll definitely survive."

I know our igloo must melt one day. But not yet. Not so soon.

"What are you thinking, Nirvana?" he asks when I'm quiet for a while.

I sigh. We've both said we'll never lie to each other. "What if we never see each other again—if we only last as long as our igloo?"

"Ah, but snow is full of paradox, isn't it? We built our igloo so well, with thick, packed snow so it can survive the heat for a long, long time."

"Mmm," I murmur, cheered up at the double meaning of what he says. "That's true, Jean-Lou."

We pause.

"We're arriving in Le Biot now," he tells me.

Where Marc and his huskies live. Where his grandparents had their winter chalet.

"Everyone else has got off—just me now to take up the mountain."

"So all the snow has gone even higher up?"

"Yep. All grey and sad at the sides of the roads."

It makes *me* feel grey and sad thinking about him going back to his mother on his own while here I fail exams right, left and centre. We'd be doing infinitely better together.

"I wish I was there," I say, "and could come to check on our igloo with you."

"Me too."

Then the front door goes, and I have to hang up fast with a whispered, *à plus tard*.

Claude comes bombing in and insists I do his new reading book with him. Afterwards, I force myself upstairs to make what are my first notes for biology. I don't even allow myself to contact Jean-Lou again all night. He doesn't contact me either.

SEVEN

WEDNESDAY AND THURSDAY morning are a blur of humiliation, with physics, biology and maths even worse than I imagined. *Chickens coming home to roost* is a saying of Nana's that would fit perfectly.

Jean-Lou's gone quiet, giving me space after my catastrophic report of the first day of exams. We've exchanged very brief WhatsApps, that's all, but once I've finished tomorrow, we'll be back to normal, I'm sure.

What's keeping me going is Sab's gonna tell me about her plans for my boards straight after English language this afternoon. After that, it's all downhill: tomorrow morning's French writing and comprehension, which I don't need to do anything about. The afternoon's for subjects scheduled against art, and my portfolio's all done and submitted for that.

English language is the only paper so far with a glimmer of hope—I get really into the science-fiction extract about a young woman who's determined to go off to live on Mars with her boyfriend and the fierce upset it causes with her mother. When the writing question is *Write a short story about a young person in conflict with a parent*, I find it flows out of me quite naturally, this time stemming from my mum and me, rather than Jean-Lou and his.

I MEET SAB outside the hall, almost jumping up and down to hear where she's found for my wood, but she just hands me a Curly Wurly and makes me wait till we're out of school.

"So," she says, finally, as we walk towards the gates, "you actually gave me the idea, Niv, with your message from the Alps about being like mountains and not hiding away."

"What you mean?" I garble through my mouthful of chocolaty toffee. "I can't risk telling Mum about the wood just yet."

"Obviously. But where better..." she pauses for dramatic effect, "than your own garage?"

I gulp, stop, turn to her.

"What?" she says. "I'm sure you said your parents never go in there?"

"They don't! Only me for the lawn mower in summer. Why didn't I think of it? Hiding in plain sight. It's outrageous! And genius!"

"That's why it took me to think of it!"

"Only one drawback," I tell her. "You're not gonna be able to come there without being spotted."

She shrugs. "It's only for a few weeks, eh? Then we'll have to face the great outdoors again."

I can't stop grinning as she tells me the plans for tomorrow afternoon. I'm still grinning even after we've gone our separate ways.

As I TURN onto Castle View, an email pings. Jean-Lou? It's not how we usually keep contact. I'm dying to tell him Sab's idea but thought he'd still be in college. I turn into the bus shelter and rest on the leaning bar while I open it.

From: CITB

My heart jolts.

Subject: Apprenticeships in Woodworking Manufacturing

Dear Nirvana Green,
Your application has been matched with the following two firms—

Matched! I'm a match! Somewhere wants me!

Winslow Wood, Manchester.

Country Kitchens, Huddersfield.

Forcing myself to slow down, I read the details again. Manchester: yes. I used to get the train to Hackspace there from Presdale. Huddersfield: awkward. Too far to go daily, too near to justify staying over.

I read on.

Using the contact details on their websites, please send off your CV and covering letter as soon as possible; portfolio evidence by 31 January. Companies will then decide whether or not to call you to interview.

That's it! So little and so much. My future in a few short lines. And thanks to Sab and her bold idea, I can get the table made in the next few weeks after all. I'm so excited, I text Mum and tell her I'll be a bit late home. Then I turn back the way I've just come, to the traffic lights, then over the road towards the Grove.

Somehow, it doesn't feel right for me to find out any more about Winslow Wood until I'm with Querky. After all, we're in this together!

Perching on my bed of planks, even though it's pretty damp under my Parka, I type the website address of Winslow Wood into my phone. Turns out they supply bespoke furniture of all types and sizes, mainly to the kitchen and bedroom industries but to individuals too.

I scroll down the menu on the top right and find 'Apprenticeships'.

They have four for September but only one in woodworking. Two days a week, you're on release to college, plus they pay £100 for the three days you work! Train fares would bite into it, but I bet I could save twenty quid each week towards going to see Jean-Lou. I don't expect my family to fund that.

I pat my plank stack. *This is really happening for us now!* Right at the bottom of Winslow Wood's webpage on apprenticeships is a bold heading: 'Requirements'.

I skim through the sentences.

Go over them more carefully, word for word.

Hold my phone at arm's length, as if that could help.

Draw my hand back in.

Every letter, every number is the same as I first thought.

Together, they squish me sideways, sick-en-ing me.

Minimum GCSE passes (level 5):

Maths
English language
At least one science.

My eyes blur. Science? Why do they need a science? Why does Winslow Wood have to be different? The word science never appeared once on the CIBT website.

I hate the CITB. And I hate friggin' elitist Winslow Wood.

Then my mouth turns bitter.

They can't be the only firm with those requirements.

As rain starts dripping wearily off branches all around me, I want to hurl my phone right across the clearing, smash it against a beech tree. To stop myself, I shove it in my pocket.

DRIZZLE WEEPS PATHETICALLY onto my shoulders as I trudge home. Mum raises her eyebrows and sighs when she sees my face.

"Physics not been great then?" she asks, making a brew in the kitchen.

I shake my head. *You don't know the half of it*, I think. I glance up at her as she leans on the Aga, looking into her mug. The rate I'm going, she'd be glad if I could actually manage to bag any apprenticeship at all.

As I get changed, I can't even face Jean-Lou. I was dying to tell him about my two apprenticeship matches—was all ready to phone him from the Grove. Till I read the fine detail.

Even *he's* going to struggle to find an upside to all this.

EIGHT

FRIDAY'S BRIGHTER RIGHT from the start and I don't just mean the weather. When I wake up, I know I can't give up my ambition, abandon what most makes me. Somehow, I've got to convince my biology teacher that I can lift my level substantially by June so she'll predict me higher.

That and keep the faith with my miner's table.

Today's French comprehension is laughably easy. Writing's simple too. Having spent all week horribly aware everyone else in the hall was doing unimaginably better than me, I finally get to feel ever so slightly smug for the first time ever in this school.

While I'm waiting for everyone else to finish, I've got too much time to think of Jean-Lou and why else he might be in touch less and less each passing day. When I think of last weekend, Monday even, and how we were constantly in each other's lives, there's no ignoring that we're down to one exchange a day now. In fact, yesterday, neither of us contacted the other in any way at all. Sometimes, you just don't want to talk about bad stuff but neither can you hide it from the one who knows you best.

At least that's how it is with me. But Jean-Lou? If it's too hard for me to talk about how badly everything's going, the same could be true for him. Yet, as he told me, we're two particles who, although separated, feel what the other is going through. My legs jiggle up and down, raring to find out. If it's her, Ghislaine, bringing him down, I should be supporting him.

I screw my eyes tight to try to banish the worst thought of all. Then I shake it out of my head. It'll all be great again this afternoon. Especially when he sees the photo I've got planned.

I move on to another painful drawer in my brain: Monday evening and the 'results debriefing' Dominique has already scheduled for when Claude's in bed. I force myself to take stock, to prepare myself.

I've got 8 in art, 9 in French; that's for sure.

If I sort out my timing, and you imagine I'd actually answered the poetry question, my English lit will be okay in the end.

Maybe English language might come out at a 4. I have to admit, though I was into it, I wasn't exactly analytical about the comprehension passage, and I didn't plan my story or remember all the language twiddly bits you're supposed to put in.

The three sciences and maths, though... I actually, genuinely shudder at how low my numbers will go. Why on earth did I predict myself a 5 for maths on the CITB registration? If that's what earned me the match with Winslow Wood...

The invigilator comes for my paper and I slam that door closed in relief.

When I meet up with Sab in the corridor, my spirits pick right up again. She's on good form, relieved to have done better than she's expected in most of her exams, which are actually over! Apart from French speaking on Monday, which I really don't need to worry about, *and*, she tells me, everything's sorted for this afternoon. My miner's table is go!

Jean-Lou'll be over the moon for me when he sees the results of her plan.

HAVING TOLD MUM I'm seeing Sab before home time, I stand us a pizza from Domingo's to take to the Grove.

Even though the track to our clearing's still sloppy with mud that very nearly comes over the top of our school shoes, it's finally stopped raining, and the sun's doing its best to warm our shoulders. Once we've scoffed our pizza, I uncover my planks. Let them breathe.

At two-thirty, I start to get edgy.

"He'll be here," Sab tells me. "No way will Alz miss out on twenty quid."

That's most of my Christmas money from Grandad.

At last, a rumble interrupts the silence of the Grove. The whirring of wheels grows reassuringly louder, like someone turning the volume up. Then we glimpse the red of the *Fit Feet Fast* van reversing down the track, churning up mucky slush on either side as it trundles down the track.

Sharp and lean as his sister, Alz nods to me as he opens the back doors.

"Plus my last fiver," I say, handing over the notes, "for the car wash."

"Cheers, Niv," he says.

First off, I haul over the two Xs of my workbench. Alz shoves them to the back. Then I spread the tarp that protected my planks across the van bottom.

JENNIFER BURKINSHAW

As Sab and I heft up the first of my boards between us to manoeuvre into the back of the van, it's like taking patients by ambulance from hospital to home.

"Gently!" I urge Alz, as he swings around the next on his own and crashes it down on top of the first. He gives me a scathing look that's a bit like one of Sab's sharp looks but without the empathy.

Once they're all in, far more haphazardly than I'd have liked, Sab clambers in the front next to him.

I set off walking the other way, fast as ever I can to check the coast is clear.

On Castle View, I bump into Mum.

"You're going early for Claude," I say.

"Hello to you too, Niv," she says. "How was French?"

"*Parfait!*"

I force myself not to jiggle or look at my phone, but I want her off Castle View, and fast.

"Where've you been?" she asks, frowning at my slutchy shoes.

"See you and Claude at home," I tell her, pretending not to have heard.

Once I'm in, I lock the front door and leave the key in the back so Mum can't get in if she's back too soon. I push off my filthy shoes and bomb straight through the house with them, down the garden and out the gate at the bottom.

Both ways up and down the puddly, shingly back street behind our row of houses are clear—of vehicles and people. Phew!

Now I can phone Sab. "Outside our garage now. Can't miss me."

"Five minutes."

186

I've had the garage key safely in my pocket since before breakfast this morning. I unlock the door, flaky with black paint. Thank goodness we never use the garage, except in summer when I get the lawn mower out through the side door in the garden. The metal mechanism groans as I pull it up till it's high enough to push up and in.

I survey the garage floor. Shoulda come and looked at this before. But when? It's grubby and dusty, but I've just got time to spread out dust sheets from the shelf onto the concrete.

My stomach lurches as, spraying up mucky water from the puddles formed in the potholes on our back street, the van comes thundering down. If only it was anything other than red! I glance up at the neighbours' windows. Thankfully, most of them are at work, but my pulse still races. This idea of Sab's is the best, the only one. But it takes some nerve, this right-under-their-very-noses plan!

Alz pulls past our garage so we can get to the van doors again.

Five minutes later, my planks are safely inside.

"We did it!" I say.

Sab grins. Alz shrugs like it's a non-event.

"We'll get gone," she says.

I nod. They must. "You're the best," I tell her.

"I know!"

"One day, I'll do something just as amazing for you, I promise."

I check my tracker. I've a good five minutes before Mum and Claude could possibly be back, so I pull down the wide door behind me.

You're home, I tell my boards.

Well, temporary, transition home, before they're finally back with Grandad, where they belong.

For now, though, their home is this dry, indoor space literally on my backdoor step. Like the Grove, it's so dangerous it's safe; the dangers are just different ones. No one comes in our garage but me anyway, and now I can slip in not only whenever the rest of them are out, but also whenever I go for a 'walk'. I'll come down the back street and into the garage that way.

I restack my planks, set up my bench and waver as I struggle to get the first one across it. Then I get my handsaw off the shelf. Last summer, when I was still allowed to go to Hackspace, I could only afford two tools. The supervisor said the indispensable ones were a plane and a saw. I take the cover off and inspect its teeth. Hardly used. I lay it on top of the board stretched across the bench and take a flash photo.

My safe, indoor space, I put on my caption to Jean-Lou. *Our garage!*

Then I've got to leg it. Lock the door. Back up the garden. I leave my shoes on the back doorstep, dash to unlock the front door. Hanging outside, I glance down Castle View: no sign of them yet. No reply from Jean-Lou yet. Grabbing some kitchen roll, I clean my shoes in the hope Mum'll forget she ever saw them in a state.

By the time Claude comes bursting in, I've put the kettle on and am sitting with Rova by the Aga. My mind's somewhere else entirely, though, half of it a hundred metres away, the other half a thousand miles away, with Jean-Lou.

NINE

OVER THE WEEKEND, reality kicks in.

It should be all my dreams come true having my timber right on the doorstep, but it's become clear I have my work cut out for me in more ways than one. Though less complex than a shepherd's table, a miner's table is so much more than a conventional table, and I only have hand tools and three weeks.

While I can get to the garage in two minutes, it's only for safe bursts of time such as when they all go off to the supermarket or the weather's fine enough to make a walk believable. If I'm to get it done, I need to be in there all day, including after dark, but I seriously doubt Mum'd let me 'walk to Sab's' and back in the evenings, or anywhere else, in fact.

I force myself to calm down, work steadily in the time I've got, making sure I get things right first time. *Measure twice, cut once*, Nana used to advise when I rushed things. Yet I do still hurry everything, that's the problem.

While I'm working on the long pieces of wood which will form the tall upright, Jean-Lou nags away at my mind. He wrote a single, matter-of-fact line on Friday night:

> *No signal over the weekend—going to Chalet Ouzon with Papa. Sorry, Nirvana.*

189

That was it. No response to my exam results; nothing about the photos of my wood in the garage. I keep trying not to take it to heart. It'll do both of them good to get away from Ghislaine. His dad must be taking some time off from the resto after all the busyness of Christmas and New Year, now it's out of season. I picture them maybe climbing to the very top of Mont Ouzon, to its cross, sitting at the shepherd's table playing chess in the evenings, and try to be glad for them.

Most of all, I wish it were me there with Jean-Lou. Yep, even if it means the table never gets finished.

I wish, in the darkest corner of my mind, I didn't have to worry he's letting me go. *Sorry, Nirvana*—is he sorry for more than being out of contact for the weekend? Maybe Sab was right, and once you're not with someone, all the feel-good fades away. For him, anyway.

Nothing to be done about it for now but keep busy, get on with my sawing whenever I can, but all the time I'm jumpy about being found out, especially whenever I have to be back in the house before the rest of my family.

Grandad comes round on Sunday, and we have one of our family afternoon teas, which is great except it stops me getting on with his table! If only I could say, "Come with me, Grandad," and show him what I'm doing. It might give him hope too, as he's in the thick of packing up his decades at Oak Vista, due to move out the very first day of February.

Come Sunday night, though, I can actually lay out and photograph for my portfolio all the components of the table—the uprights, tabletop, even the supporting leg.

Not bad going, after all, Niv, under the circumstances. Tomorrow, though.

Tomorrow, Jean-Lou will have to be back down in the village to get the school bus, so he'll be in touch first thing.

Tomorrow I get my mock results.

The verdict'll be in. On both vital parts of my life.

I WAKE UP clutching my phone. Because Jean-Lou's an hour ahead of me, I can't miss his call or message. I'm still clasping it as I eat my toast one-handed.

As Ms. Settle walks in with a big stack of our exam scripts, I turn my phone to vibrate. I'm ever more anxious about Jean-Lou. Something's not right.

There's a '4' in green at the top of my English lit paper. I breath out, astounded it's no lower, when I missed out a third of the paper. Sab looks at me across the aisle, holding up four fingers. I force myself to read the 'How to Improve' comment:

> Actually answer the poetry question and a 6
> is well within your grasp, Nirvana — a very
> engaged answer on East of Eden and an
> interesting response to R and J!

Mechanically, I write down everything Ms. Settle says as she goes through the paper, even though my mind's in France, wondering what's going on with Jean-Lou. I try to feel cross with him for not being in touch this morning, but I can't. Don't think I ever could. My heart's *uneasy* about him, exactly as if, as he said about particles, what's affecting him is also affecting me.

In English language, the one which counts most for my apprenticeship, I actually get a 5!

On my lap, I WhatsApp Jean-Lou with my rare, good news.

No reply.

TEN

A T BREAK, I sit in the canteen on my own, glued to my phone.

Sab comes back from her French oral part way through.

"It were that bad," she huffs, "I didn't dare meet Hazy's eye in case we both started laughing. A right *Lost in Translation* sit!"

I chuckle, in spite of everything. If chem is my write-off, French is Sab's. Maybe we should all be allowed a write-off. Even some of the smuggos sitting all around us in the canteen have had to drop art, for example. My French oral's last thing.

STILL NOTHING FROM Jean-Lou by the time I go into maths, which is when the day starts to tip violently downhill.

> Maths: 4
> Chemistry: 3
> Physics: 3
> Biology: 4

I'm appalled by my results. Until the end of Year 9, I did pretty well at school. Then I started to lose focus more and more, wishing I was outside or at least doing something practical. But even I didn't know I'd let things get to this stage—the stage where I've jeopardised my apprenticeship.

I message Jean-Lou, giving him the whole sorry list, including that low numbers are bad, in the hope it might trigger a response. And a bit of sympathy, actually.

As I SIT waiting for my turn outside Monsieur Hayes' office, I should be looking forward to something I can finally ace. Monsieur Hayes is one of my favourite teachers. He's kind and what everyone calls hazy, or vague, hence his nickname. I reckon it's more that his mind's full of interesting stuff that he can't allow out because he's got to make himself stick to the syllabus and teach us irregular verbs. Like Claude, he's got one English and one French parent, so at least his French is real. If it wasn't, Dominique would have banned French GCSE. I'm not kidding.

Because I've still heard nothing from Jean-Lou, though, speaking French is the last thing I want to be doing. I'm going to have to face up to the very real possibility that he really is dropping me and in the worst possible way.

Need to be out of here, I think, looking to the glass door at the end of the corridor, even though it's grey and miserable.

Jaz jaunts out of Hazy's office and flicks her glossy hair as she passes me. I so wish I'd stuck my foot out.

"*Entre*, Nirvana!" Monsieur Hayes says.

My heart smarts at the mellowness of his voice, the way he says my name, careful, unlike Dominique. Like Jean-Lou. I'd give *anything* to hear my name in his mouth again.

I swallow, breathe, get a grip. This is just a bit of a chat that happens to be in French.

Which is, of course, the whole problem.

Monsieur Hayes starts up with a bit of a warm-up about this being my last exam. Then he looks down at his desk to pick one of the set topics.

"*Alors,* Nirvana," he says, smiling to put me ease. "What have you done during the Christmas holidays?"

I huff out a little and look at my lap; press my lips together tightly. It'd be so easy to tell Monsieur Hayes the whole truth.

I met a lad who felt like the best friend I'd ever have, then we kissed and it was so much more. But now he's gone quiet on me, and I don't know why.

"Did you stay at home or go away?" Monsieur Hayes gently prompts.

I take a deep breath and tell him the official version. "It was a surprise, but we went to France to ski. We stayed in a chalet. I had some ski lessons. I tried food I had never eaten before, such as tartiflette and fondue. It snowed all the time, but I did once get to see the view of all the mountains, including Mont Blanc."

Igloo's a word I can't use.

It's so vivid in my head, I'm back there. My heart stings all over again. If I were there with Jean-Lou, everything would be all right. I know it would.

Monsieur Hayes asks me one or two questions about where we flew to and how I like skiing—I willingly tell him the whole truth on these ones—then it's all over.

Out in the corridor, he tells me how super my accent is and that I've done really well. I try to look pleased, but he's still talking to me in French and it's making me want to cry.

THE WEATHER'S TEARY too, so I can't find any credible excuse to get outside and around to the garage to do the one thing that would have distracted me a little, as well as urgently needing to be done.

In the kitchen, Mum peers at me as she hands me a brew, assessing how bad my results are. I'm not going through that twice, though. She can wait for the emergency COBRA meeting with Dominique later. Not that I need any debriefing to know how humongously I've sabotaged not only my own career but my chances of seeing Jean-Lou again. Now I've not a leg to stand on, not a hope in hell—if I ever work up the nerve to bring him up.

Worst of all, a terrifyingly dark and expanding corner of my mind tells me, he might not want to come anymore anyway.

I volunteer to tell Claude his bedtime story. Being with my little brother or Rova are the only bits of relief just now. If I read Claude right to the end of *Billy and the Minpins*, maybe we can skip the torture of the post-exam debrief altogether.

"Nirvan-ah!" Dominique yells at 7:35.

"Just finishing the chapt-ah!" I yell back.

Claude sniggers, making me smile for the first time today.

"You'd better go, Niv," he says.

"Is there anything you don't know about?"

He shakes his head sadly.

I bat his curls with the *Minpins* book and turn his light out.

"*Courage!*" he repeats, just a little bit sleepily.

ELEVEN

"A LORS," DOMINIQUE SAYS at our round kitchen table. In Mum's place is a pad of lined paper on which my GCSE subjects are listed.

She puts a brew in front of us both then a plate of chocolate digestives. I help myself at once.

They both sit back and wait for me to speak. If only I had a call with Jean-Lou to look forward to and wasn't totally on my own against them, I'd get through this.

I draw myself up on my chair. "I'll start with the good news then."

So, I start with French, remind them of my 8 in art too, and make Mum add them to her incomplete list.

Then I go through the promising parts: English and English language.

I reach for another—absolutely crucial—biccie.

"Maths, Niv," Mum prompts.

Looking at the tabletop, with all its scratches from years of me and Claude, I garble the number through my mouthful.

She doesn't look remotely surprised as she writes it down.

"And the sciences?" Dominique asks.

I mumble the pitifully low numbers.

Silence. The silence of disapproval and disappointment. They exchange disbelieving glances across the table.

If they'd leapt to their feet shouting, "What the *!$#?"
it'd be infinitely easier.

"These are so far below the levels you used to achieve,"
Mum says at last. "What *have* you been doing with your
time, Niv?"

"Well, I've been being ripped away on a skiing holiday
right before my mocks for one thing!"

"Was that really the problem?" Dominique asks, her
face wrinkling in a rare stricken moment.

Mum looks at me hard.

"No," I mutter looking down at my hands.

"What then?" Mum says.

"I'm in the wrong place doing the wrong things," I say
miserably.

She claps her hands on the table. "Niv, everyone has
to do GCSEs. That's how it is. What *are* we going to do
with you?"

My mouth turns down. Nothing. I'm a lost cause. I've
bombed my mocks

thrown away my apprenticeship

and it's looking increasingly like I've lost my Jean-Lou.
Still nothing from him since *Friday*, and now it's almost the
end of the day, when he must be long back from collège.

"Don't give up, *chou-chou*," Dominique says, astounding
me. "You just need the right support with maths
and science."

I nod and look at my lap. If I look at her, tears will
spill over.

"I need some air," Mum says, taking Rova with her to
the garden.

Dominique's hand slides across the table towards me. "Your mum only needs to...cool off for a minute, Nirvan-ah."

It's nice of her, but I can't help wondering if she'd be so relaxed if it was Claude, her own flesh and blood, who was messing up his life.

Have I totally messed it up? My English language is okay. Maybe, if I go to Maths Club and promise to get tuition, Ms. Bailey could be persuaded to predict me a 5. Then, if I focused just on biology, I reckon I could get a 5 in that too.

I need to tell Mum and Dominique about this opportunity I've got with Winslow Wood and the miner's table ready to take shape not so far away. I visualise it, complete: Querky's gold-flecked grain in a bespoke piece of furniture for Grandad. That will really prove it to them at the end of the month.

The back door opens, and Rova scrambles up the step.

"WELL, NIRVANA," MUM says, hands on her hips, eyes burning into me. "Rova sniffed out how you've been wasting all your time." She shifts her eyes to Dominique. "Creating chaos in the garage."

I leap up, pulse thumping in my ears. "I haven't been wasting my time. And that chaos, as you call it, that's a table for *my* grandad, made from his own tree."

"That was taken to Hackspace," Mum says, her face all scrunched up.

"Yeah, well, I wasn't allowed to go there anymore, was I? So now it's here."

"You have been in the garage instead of revising all these months?" Dominique asks, looking between the two of us, bewildered.

I panic. I'm not ready for this. It'd save me explaining where else I've been—and when—to let them think I *was* in the garage all along.

"Well, have you?" Mum urges, stepping nearer.

"No," I say, after all. Time for truth now. "The boards only arrived on Friday. After all the exams."

The tension subsides. Just a fraction. Dominique even nods.

Mum and I stand suspended on this fragile rope. If she doesn't ask any more questions about hows and wheres, I might even get through the next few minutes.

"It's not just for Grandad either," I say, breaking the impasse. "The table will double count—for my apprenticeship too."

The word lights the blue touch paper.

"I knew it!" Mum says, actually shaking her finger at me. "I knew there was something behind this, this…this…"

She snatches her pad from the table and brandishes it.

"These…are all you need to be an apprentice?" she says, scathing. She turns to Dominique, who's getting to her feet in alarm. "Low expectations, that's what this is all about."

"What this is about," I tell her, my voice loud and wavery, "is *wrong* expectations. Yours. I'm not the daughter you wanted. Well, tough. This is me."

I push past her, out to the garden, where a rhombus of light shines onto the lawn from the garage side door.

Slamming it behind me, I sink down against it, knees to chest, head low.

200

TWELVE

BEYOND TEARS, MY body's so chockful of hurt I don't know what to do to release its buzzing. Adrenalin, I suppose. I gaze at the boards in front of me, on which all the hopes for my future are nailed and the rest of the stuff scattered around the garage. If I'd been more organised, disciplined, it would have looked more...professional. Fact is, I can't even do this. I've been kidding myself that I could actually construct a table.

Mum's right. I've been wasting my time. Here and everywhere.

I *am* a com-plete
ut-ter
waste of time.

I thought I could be *something*—someone with a craft to be proud of, someone worthy of Jean-Lou.

I'm so humiliated, I can't bring myself to put it into words to Sab, Rova or anyone else on this planet. My nana, she'd have been the only one. What an unholy mess I've made of my future, failing the science it turns out I need to be an apprentice. I've blocked my own route to being me, no help from Mum necessary.

With no one left to turn to, my thoughts slide to my donor dad. Why wait two years to find his identity when

I need him ASAP? I've read true stories on the net of genetic tests that can help you trace your donor family.

But then what if *he's* a waste of space, like me, confirming all Mum's said?

Or doesn't want to know me?

I rock back and forth, lost.

I need *someone* who believes in me. And now.

Sab. She's been an unbeatable friend this week. Far more than I deserve.

But I can't face Mum again. Not even tomorrow.

Suddenly, it's clear as ice what I must do.

ONCE THE LIGHT goes off in the kitchen, I close up the garage and sneak inside and upstairs. The telly's blaring from the living room, that's how much they care!

I empty my backpack, replace the schoolbooks with a few clothes. Then I turn my light out way before they come up for bed so they don't come to say goodnight— as if they would!

Half an hour later, I creep back downstairs, avoiding the creaky steps.

In the kitchen, I find Mum's handbag hanging on the back of the chair she was sitting on earlier. I sit where she sat, bag on my knee. Rifling through your mum's handbag for her purse is as low as it gets.

But desperate times, desperate measures.

As I pilfer the £30 in notes and type her credit card number into the Easy Jet checkout, I want to think Mum's pushed me into this or that I'm doing it only for

Jean-Lou. I *do* need to see him. I've got to know he's all right. *We're* all right. It's impossible to wait any longer to hear from him.

But I also know, underneath it all, it's for me too. I've nowhere left to go.

The page of my shameful results is still lurking on the kitchen table. I pick up the pen and add to the bottom:

I'm really sorry — will replace all the money. Please don't worry or call the police. I'll be safe. Will be in touch and back soon. There is something I have to do. Niv

I thumb a short message to Jean-Lou and kill my phone, stuff it in one pocket, the cash in the other. Then I crouch down by Rova, deeply asleep with her back against the Aga.

"Take care, my sweetheart," I tell her, rubbing my face in the scruff of her neck. "Love you."

I pad into the front room and find my passport in the sideboard drawer.

In the hall, I root out my ski jacket from under all the others and check the inside zip pocket. Thank God— the twenty-euro note left over from my holiday spending money from Grandad is still there. And yes! My gloves are in the pockets.

In the porch, my snow boots, where I left them the day we got home, are ice-cold.

But I'm off, closing the front door gently behind me.

AT THE GATE, I turn left.

Through the empty streets I stride, but I'm not scared. Nobody can stop me tonight. Even the rain's given up for me.

I'm almost ten minutes early for the train. The machine on the platform doesn't take cash, so I'm gonna have to risk getting on without a ticket.

At Manchester airport, I have to switch my phone back on for the boarding card on my app. Once I've scanned it, I check for a reply from Jean-Lou. An hour ahead, he must have already been asleep when I sent my message. *I'm turning my phone off now till I'm with Jean-Lou*, I vow, just in case Mum finds my message before morning and has the police track me.

Once I've had my backpack scanned, I find a row of cushioned chairs in the quietest spot. Then, using my pack as a pillow, I try to settle to sleep: it's four loooong hours before the gate opens when all I want is to be there.

But the second I shut my eyes, all I can think is

What have you gone and done now, Niv?

The last few hours feel like something out of a film, part of a life of some character who isn't me. Only I bet even Sab couldn't think of a film that reflects my life right now.

In stealing from my own mother, in running away, I've turned an almighty mess into one that's off the Richter Scale.

Would I be doing this but for my very real worries for Jean-Lou?

No.

Would I be doing it but for the fiasco that's my life?

No again.

Whatever, I tell myself. *No turning back now*. And I wouldn't want to. I just have to face up to the fact that what I'm doing's going to make everything exponentially worse at home and could even risk mine and Jean-Lou's hopes of seeing each other again in the future.

Then I picture his mother's dead eyes. Am I really going to subject myself to her and her scorn? And am I just going to make everything even worse for him?

Despite everything, including Ghislaine, and especially my fear we're over before we've really got going, something's still compelling me to get to him.

I must have fallen asleep because one of those round floor polishers wakes me up, the cleaner jolting my section of seats. Having unfurled my achy body, I take unsteady steps towards the flight board.

My heart trips. 3:10 a.m. My gate's already up, the flight on time.

I go to the tall windows. An Easy Jet plane's coming in to land. The runways are quiet, so it's very likely my plane!

My teeth are bumpy, my mouth bitter, so I dash to the toilets and have a very quick clean.

And I'm boarding!

My pulse beats faster the nearer I get to the front of the queue, like someone's going to stop me, turn me back. It's not impossible, if Mum or Dominique have been into my room for some reason and found me missing. But the only way they could think of the Alps is if they asked Sab for ideas, and she wouldn't give me away.

The official scans my pass, glances at my passport, no problem. Next thing I know, I'm on the plane, over the wing.

I turn my phone off now till I get to Ouzon. Just in case my parents try tracking me.

Come on, come on I urge the plane. *Let's be off!*

Then the engines power up, and the huge metal bird trundles out to its runway, hovers like it's working up the nerve to do some sort of massive run...which it is. The pilot throttles back and goes for it. The nose leaves the earth.

I'm doing this, actually doing it! A right Great Escape!

PART III:
11 JANUARY

ONE

TOO EDGY TO sleep, I open up the Montaigne book I downloaded on my eReader when I first got home from France and find the essay *On Friendship* in the index, the bit Jean-Lou was telling me they read in collège on Monday. Montaigne writes about four different kinds of love, including romantic, but it's friendship, he says, is the most important relationship of his life. True friendship, he claims, is higher than any other kind of love, a spiritual mixing of two into one piece with no sign of a seam.

Then my heart jumps. Montaigne finishes by writing about him and his pal de Boetie: 'True friendship is for no reason other than because it is you, because it is I.' That's the phrase Jean-Lou used for him and me. We *are*...inevitable.

For the first time since I walked out our front gate, I'm positive I'm doing the right thing.

As the plane starts to tilt down, I haven't slept for one minute of the sixty it's taken so far. Now I'm away from England, I can look forward.

I'm seeing Jean-Lou in just a couple of hours! I messaged him to say I was coming, so he could well be there to meet me.

It's still dark, obviously, but as we get lower, the white Jura Mountains come into view, lower, less jagged than the Alps.

The lights of Geneva are ahead, so we must be flying over the croissant lake Jean-Lou and I saw only a couple of weeks ago from La Pointe du Mont.

As soon as we've landed and the seat-belt signs are off, I stand. It's pointless when I'm in the middle of the plane, but I can't stop myself.

I watch both the front and back exits to see which is emptying faster. Once I'm off, at the rear, I stand for a second, taking in the pure air of Switzerland. Then I dash down, scoot around everyone, bomb for passport control. At least I know where I'm going.

The border officer barely glances at my passport. I pelt through the marble, underground corridors, through Duty Free, past Baggage Reclaim, to the exit. I can hardly breathe. This could so be one of those dramatic lovers-reunite situations. Then again, it could be excruciating awkwardness if Jean-Louis feels obliged to meet me, only to tell me to get on the next flight back because we're over already, not inevitable after all.

The doors slide open and I step through, scan the faces of the twenty or thirty people there.

Not one of them is here to welcome me. Maybe Jean-Lou didn't check his messages last night.

I swallow and look at my phone. I still daren't turn it on in the remote chance Mum found my note last night, did call the police and is having me tracked. I won't be stopped till I sort this out with Jean-Lou. Instead, I stride outside, to the pick-up area, study all the cars awaiting passengers. Maybe Monsieur Jaboulay is waiting out here for me somewhere.

I wait till everyone has dispersed.

Till not one car is left.

But it's still early, entirely possible Jean-Lou hasn't even woken up and looked at his phone yet.

I go back inside.

It's empty too. Opposite the exit doors I came through, there's an information desk, but it's not yet open, not for another *two* hours! I walk down the corridor to the right of where I came out into Arrivals, past about six different car hire desks. Only two are open. Then it hits me: loads of people on my plane were skiers, wearing padded trousers, and one man even ski boots, to save room in their cases. Surely some of them are hiring cars?

I leg it down the rest of the corridor to where the rental cars are parked. Yes! Just one, an estate car, is backing out of a space. I dash ahead of it, to the open barrier at the exit, stand there with my thumb out, smiling.

Come on, stop! Stop for me, I will it as the car gets nearer and I count three heads inside, all young blokes. And yes, I'd even get in with them.

The driver winds down his window. "Where you going, love?"

He shakes his head when I tell him. They're headed to a Swiss resort.

My heart sinks as I realise I've missed whatever other car rentals there could have been. I trudge back inside, trying to ignore the acid despair steadily rising in my stomach.

As I turn the corner back to the arrival doors, my heart rises in one desperate last hope that maybe, just maybe, Jean-Lou'll be here now, just a bit late.

The whole area's completely deserted.

So what's next, Niv?

In the opposite direction, is a sign, 'Ski Navettes'.

I follow it like it's a star.

My heart jumps as I spot another sign: 'Alpine bus'.

And a person manning the little podium desk. Nearby, near the sliding exit doors, there are more people: a small group waiting for the bus.

I race to the desk. It takes at least two minutes for the guy to stop looking at his phone long enough to give me a bored look.

"*Bonjour*," I say brightly. "I am looking for a shuttle to Le Biot, on the Morzine route, please."

He jabs his finger at a laminated sign I'd not seen, stuck to the left of the lectern thing: *Pre-booked tickets only*.

My pulse picks up. *Do you have any idea*, I want to scream at him, *how much I need to get to Jean-Lou?*

"Is there a shuttle to Morzine?" I ask him.

"Again," he says, jabbing his hand at the sign again.

"Yes, but if you have a seat empty on the bus, why could I not buy it now?"

"*Desolé*," he says, anything but sorry. "We have no means of taking payment except online."

I put my hand on the desk. Right, so after coming hundreds of miles, I can't make the last thirty? I stare at him. He glares at my hand on his desk until I shift it. Then he's back on his phone. Immovable. A real, live jobsworth, as Grandad would call him. Rules are rules, it seems, especially in Switzerland.

I lope across the corridor and sink down the wall.

I pull my knees into my chest and bury my face in them.

Now what?

A waft of icy air stirs me. The little group is going out of the sliding doors. I flick a glance at Jobsworth—still on his phone—and follow them out.

I zip around to the front. Morzine! This minibus, which must seat twelve or fifteen, is actually going to Morzine! I count the group—seven of them taking their luggage to the rear doors of the navette.

I lurk by the passenger door, my heart pounding in my ears. Do I just get on and risk it, or...come clean.

"No luggage?" the driver asks me.

I shake my head. My right foot's actually on the bottom step of the minibus. Whether or not this goes via Le Biot, I'm getting on it. Morzine's so much nearer.

"Booking confirmation, please?" she asks.

TWO

Now I KNOW how the two men in *The Great Escape* felt, when, right on the brink of pulling off their breakout, they're caught out at the very last second.

Can I pretend I've not heard?

I sigh, put my foot back down, turn to face this woman. She has cool, blue eyes that remind me of Dominique's. This is who stands between me and Jean-Lou.

I swallow. Root in my inner pocket.

"I have this." I hold out my twenty-euro note to her.

"Online bookings only," she raps out and turns away.

"I know," I say. "But please..."

She's starting to clamber into the driving seat.

I scrabble after her, grab the door.

"Please," I say. "I am *toute seule*." All alone sounds more emotive in French. "I am sixteen and have to get to someone in Le Biot. I have nowhere else to go. And I only have this."

I wave my note at her, my voice wavering. But I won't cry.

The others are all in the bus now, waiting.

She glances over her shoulder at them.

Look at all those empty seats! I will her.

She jerks her head. "Get in."

I beam at her, my favourite person on the planet at this moment.

My hand goes to my heart. *"Merci,"* I say in the hugest of understatements.

Nothing can stop me now, nothing can stop me, I chant to myself as the minibus passes under the barrier out of the airport.

THE SUN'S JUST rising over the Swiss mountains opposite as we ride right alongside the lake. Once we cross the border into France, rays glancing off the water, the sky's already soft blue.

My heart twitches as we pass the sign that tells us we're entering the town of Thonon. This is where Jean-Lou comes to collège. I gnaw at my finger. He won't be coming down here today, will he? Surely if I'm missing school, he can too. He'll be waiting for me in Ouzon. Won't he?

What if he's not? Maybe, for some reason, he didn't get my message. What if my shuttle actually crosses paths with his school bus? It'd be about this time he'd be arriving from the mountains, as collège starts soon after eight.

A shiver ripples down my shoulders, even in my ski jacket. If Jean-Lou is going to collège today, he really doesn't want to see me anymore. But that's impossible. I *know* how he felt. He *chose* to email me in the first place. And he said only a few days ago how we'd built not only our igloo but also us *to last*. Both of us realised how difficult it was going to be at such a distance, but we agreed: we'd rather that than give each other up.

So what's changed?

Has he met someone at collège? Someone who lives in the same country? Someone cleverer than me?

Pulling my feet up onto the seat, I hide my face in my knees again.

I don't untuck my head until, out the other side of the town, we veer inland, taking the route Jean-Lou must take every day back to Ouzon. And there they are! The dramatic, white mountains we saw from la Pointe du Mont. Before I botched every single aspect of my life.

Except this one. Whatever's going on, I'm not going home till I find out where I stand.

Now I've got to think about the next bit. I've given up hope that Monsieur Jaboulay and Jean-Lou will be waiting for me where the bus stops in Le Biot. I'm going to have to walk all the way up the mountain road to Ouzon. That'll take me a good hour. And not only is my stomach rumbling, but I feel really weak.

THE MINIBUS TURNS up from the straight, wide road into the narrow, winding valley with its steep, rocky sides looming over us, casting us in shadow inside the bus. We're slowly gaining height, and as we do, snow starts to appear at the sides of the road, grey from the mud and grit of traffic.

I start to recognise landmarks—a winter caravan park, a church.

At last, we make a left turn, off the main road and up towards Le Biot. Soon, we pass the *fromagerie* I stopped at with my family only three weeks ago. So much has happened since then, none of it good if Jean-Lou has given up on us.

I edge out into the aisle to look up ahead, craning my neck, desperate to see a tall figure.

The driver pulls up right in the middle, next to the war memorial and near the town hall. She gets out to open the back door for the other passengers. I scramble out next, peer in all directions.

Apart from our minibus, the village is deserted.

Tugging suitcases like reluctant dogs behind them, the seven other passengers disappear down a side road.

The driver closes the back doors and comes back around to the front. She gives me a look, like she regrets ever getting lumbered with me.

"No one here for you?"

I pull in my top lip and study my boots.

"Where next then?"

I look up. "Ouzon."

"Get in!" She dangles her keys. "No passengers for Morzine this morning. I can take you up in the time I would have spent going there."

I gasp and leap back inside before she changes her mind.

THREE

THE HIGHER WE get, the more snow is stacked at the sides of the roads, the faster my pulse beats, pumping in my ears. What if Jean-Lou's not there? Or his dad? Only his monster mother?

The hour plus it'd have taken me is done in ten minutes. I repeat my thanks to the driver, trying to keep my voice steady.

As she heads back down the mountain, I'm on my own in the empty car park.

Ouzon's a whole new place. I stand blinking at the brilliant white, jagged mountains under orange sun and pure azure sky. In complete contrast to a fortnight ago, everything is clear.

Too clear.

Bang in front of me is the blue piste our first igloo was at the top of. My heart twinges.

The snow is beautifully combed for the first skiers of the day, and an attendant is busy shovelling by the lift pulls, to make it easier for skiers. Unfortunately, it's not her, not Ghislaine. She must be in the resto. Or the flat. I turn my head to look up at its balcony and patio doors, overlooking the car park.

Nothing. No one to be seen.

Then I swivel right around towards the chalet we rented over Christmas. Smoke's spiralling from the chimney and a different car's on the drive.

The village has moved on, become other people's.

Maybe Jean-Lou's moved on too.

Next, I turn to Toblerone Wood in the distance. Beyond it, and up, is our igloo.

Fearful of what I will or won't find, I finally allow my eyes to come back to the resto.

Forcing my legs forward, past the ski rack, I trudge towards the front door. I stop dead. Where the path should have been is just snow, calf-deep if you walked up it. Monsieur Jaboulay's clearly not been near it today: it's nearly eight-thirty now, and the resto is as dark, as closed up as if it had been shut down.

My heart falters. *Has* it? Has something happened? Why wouldn't Jean-Lou have told me?

I do actually go up the not-path in the hope there's some sign, some message on the door. Nothing. I peer through into the gloomy interior. The chairs are stacked on the tables as they usually are in the morning, but there's no sign of life.

Then I remember. There's a back door too, though it's not one we ever used. I traipse back down the path, back to the car park and around towards the green piste. Here too, the snow is untouched, but I try the door anyway, thump on it with the side of my fist. Again and again.

I know no one's here. It *feels* dead.

Now I *have* to turn my phone on.

My hopes leap. There are two texts:

Welcome to Switzerland, the rate is...
Welcome to France, the rate is...

I deflate again.

No WhatsApp.

No missed calls.

Email? Nothing new.

Mum's not discovered I've gone yet, but nothing from Jean-Louis either.

Loathing my phone, I turn it off again and thrust it in my pocket.

I turn my back to the door. Slump against it.

So, I messaged Jean-Louis I'm arriving this morning. He and his whole family clears out.

The answer couldn't be louder.

The end of the road.

Never mind that his parents are also not here, Jean-Louis doesn't want to see me. Not enough to even miss a day of college or even to tell me in person we're over.

I'm on my own, facing a future without Jean-Lou.

My middle-of-the-night flight's going to be yet another humiliation. An hour behind in the UK, it'll be about now Mum'll find out I'm missing, discover my pathetic note as she puts out the breakfast things.

If I had any tiny chance left of salvaging my apprenticeship, I've tossed it away on this ridiculous bolting to Jean-Louis when he's not even got the decency to see me. Now, somehow, I'm going to have to get myself back to Geneva, phone Mum, get her to buy me a return ticket.

For the first time ever, I'm angry with Jean-Lou. We had an understanding. Didn't we? I staked everything on that. On his honesty. If it wasn't working for him, he should have had the guts to tell me, not this switch from hot to cool to nothing at all.

Not only is my heart broken, not only have I totally disgraced myself, I've also made everything a myriad times worse at home by standing by us. Yet another screw-up to add to my ever-longer list of failures.

Apprenticeship, relationship—both dead. Dead before they've even had a life. Worst of all is this sickening, out-of-sync-with-myself sensation in my head. I've read him all wrong and can't even trust myself anymore.

Nirvana Green, misfit extraordinaire.

A WAN WARMTH washes onto my face. I open my eyes just as the sun struggles to show the top of its head over La Pointe du Mont. I straighten up. No way! No way am I slinking home, tail between my legs. Not yet. Whatever's going on with Jean-Louis, whatever he's thinking about me, us, I'm not going till I have it out with him. He doesn't get off the hook by ignoring me. He doesn't get to treat me this way. I'm gonna sit it out till he's back from collège, come back to the resto and make him tell me to my face.

Using the deep indentations I've made in the snow like stepping stones, I tramp back to the car park. Passing in front of the resto now, I trudge down the car park on the other side of it. At the end of it, I tip down onto the edge of the beginners' piste. Some little French school kids, not much older than Claude, are enjoying flying

221

down it on this perfect skiing day, the like of which we never saw when we were here.

The route up to Toblerone Wood is all compacted into corduroy ridges I'm the first to walk on, making it easy. The stripes continue right through the wood to the other side. I'm marching it out to get through the trees fast. This lovely place is painful with memories of being here with Jean-Lou, especially our last, magical night.

I don't stop till I'm out of the trees at the other end of the path. Standing at the junction, I breathe in the air so cold it smells, tastes dry. The wide piste falling away below me is empty of skiers now. Maybe the school kids'll progress to this one next.

I turn right, up the steep track into the forest proper. Towards our igloo.

Maybe things will feel better there.

But how can they, without him?

No footprints to be seen in this direction. Jean-Lou's certainly not been to check on our igloo since he got back from Chalet Ouzon.

After about ten minutes, I start peering into the thick-packed trees for the animal track to the fallen tree and our igloo, but I can't make out the break in the trees we usually take. I decide to press on, just go a little further up in case that looks familiar.

A voice stops me dead.

I spin around.

A dark figure's striding uphill towards me.

FOUR

MY HEARTBEAT GOES haywire.

Where were you? I'm poised to shout at Jean-Lou. But he's here now! What do I do?

I stand, just stand; wait for him to come to me.

As he comes into focus, his shoulders all hunched over, it stabs at my heart.

"Nirvana!" he calls as soon as we're in earshot. "I only just got your message. What are you doing here?"

I go weak with relief. Of course he wouldn't let me down!

His voice, though... Even though he's clearly surprised, it's flat, lost all its usual bounce.

As he gets nearer, I smile at him, but he doesn't return it. He stops in front of me, slightly out of breath. We stand awkwardly, him looking beyond me somehow.

I've made the biggest embarrassment possible of myself. He doesn't want to see me after all.

I look into his face. He's pale, dark rings under his eyes. It dawns on me, if he's only just got my message, he was already not going to collège. Something's wrong. Not just me.

Suddenly, he folds over into me, heavy, his head buried in my shoulder. I stroke whatever parts of him

I can reach, till he straightens up again, still unable to meet my eye.

"To our igloo?" I ask.

We walk side by side back downhill a little, till he leads the way onto the horizontal track I missed, into the depths of the trees. As we plod single file through the untrodden snow, Jean-Lou's movements are weary, like he barely has the energy for it.

Slowly, slowly, we reach our landmark, the fallen tree.

A little further on, it's just as I've been seeing it in my head all this time.

We stand and gaze at our igloo, as we did that first afternoon we built it, spangled now in the fresh morning sun.

"It's the same as ever," I tell him.

He nods as if hardly able to believe it himself.

ONCE WE'RE IN our old positions, he unzips his backpack and offers me some water. I gulp half the bottle down before handing it back.

A moment, then I take a breath, brace myself.

"What's happened, Jean-Lou?"

He shakes his head, sighs as his shoulders drop, gathers himself.

"We stayed a third night up at the chalet. I only got your message when we came back into the village just now. Papa was going to take me to collège late..."

The painful knots in my chest slacken a little, even though that's not the whole story and doesn't explain the state he's in.

He glugs some water. I know that feeling of wanting to talk of anything except the painful stuff, but our igloo's thick walls will shield us. Its curves will soften whatever he's going to tell me.

"She's gone," he says, staring towards the igloo entrance.

My heart pauses. "Your mother?"

He nods, still looking down.

Thank God, I think, sitting very still, so he'll carry on.

"Things got worse and worse between us every passing day last week."

I feel a thud of guilt in my stomach.

"It...it wasn't because of me?"

He shakes his head firmly but doesn't say what it was about.

"My dad, he finally saw exactly what she is. And he said, 'Enough.'"

At last.

"So she just went?"

He rubs his cheek with his hand, shakes his head.

"She actually cried. The first time I've ever seen it."

I blink, several times. So she could change, after all?

"She says she wants to stay. And I think, I hope, she now realises what...who, she'd be losing.

"But Papa says no, it's too late. And then..." He clicks his fingers as he raises his eyes to mine. "She just flicks back. Crocodile tears."

Yep, that sounds more like the woman I saw too much of a couple of weeks ago. Toying with Jean-Lou's feelings, battering his heart yet again.

"She starts to shout, 'This is my home!' even though she hates it here."

He falters. "She says it's me who should go. Not her."

My blood runs cold, it really does. I reach out for his gloved hand.

"So how…?" I ask.

He hesitates, musters a sad little smile. "My father's disgusted. I've never seen him so angry. He offers her money. To be rid of her. By the end of the weekend, while Papa and I are at the chalet, she has to be gone, he tells her. Her and all her possessions."

Something like a divorce settlement? I'd pay to be free of her too!

"She pushes up her price like an auction," Jean-Lou is saying. "Even though she's never worked even a day in the resto, she knows it's made money. Finally, Papa would go no further and…" He pauses. "She accepted this amount. This large amount."

I shake my head, disgusted at her greed, and shuffle a little nearer to him.

"So, she's really gone," I sum up, still taking all this in.

He nods and meets my eyes for the first time.

"It should be good news, shouldn't it, Nirvana?" He echoes my thinking. "But yesterday, I couldn't bear to come home. If she was still here, bad news. If she'd gone… also bad news."

I ache for him, the part of him that still hoped for his relationship with his mother, that his dad's ultimatum might shake her into finally appreciating her son.

I wrap my other hand around his.

"She was, still is your mother. And now, it seems…"

I can't bring myself to say it: she never will accept him. "There's no hope," he finishes for me.

I tighten my hands on his. Maybe she couldn't help it; was never going to change, if Mum was right about her personality. What I think most of all, I can't say—that he's better off without her. He is. But first, he needs to get over the shock of her absence.

"For you, though, you and your dad, there's loads of hope, Jean-Lou," I say instead. "Once you've…adjusted."

He glances to the side, towards the village. "Papa's at the flat now, checking she's not left anything behind."

I squeeze my eyes closed. So hard. It might seem so unlike helping Grandad pack up Nana's things to dispose of them in different ways, but it's still a grieving for what Jean-Lou will never have.

"Can I help?" I ask.

In his weak smile, I get a glimpse of the old him. "You already have, Nirvana. You came."

So this is one thing I didn't get wrong? My small smile feels unfamiliar on my cheeks.

"How did you know to come?" he asks.

I stall. What's the truth? Because we said we'd always be honest.

"I sensed something was wrong."

I don't add 'between us'. That can only be secondary to him, after all he's been through. Yet, now I've heard him out, I'm aware again of *my* hurt; how he's not replied to me when I needed him, even if my troubles weren't, *aren't* as important as his.

"But also, Jean-Louis," he looks up at me when I use his full name, surprise in his eyes. "I've been having a *bad* time too." I'm going really slowly, having to search for the right words in English before putting them into French. "Not as hard as you, but like you, I struggle to be in contact as much when things are difficult. But unless impossible, I would always reply to you. Because when you're so...warm, then suddenly nothing, I don't know how we...are."

I trail off, not knowing the French for 'how things stand between us'.

He blinks, his mouth turned down. He's got the gist.

"I'm sorry, Nirvana, truly," he says, looking at the igloo floor now, then back up again. "I admit, I've only read your last message. I was totally...absorbed in myself. Tell, me, please, about this bad time."

Oh! So it's nothing to do with *me* at all that he's not been in touch!

I tell him now in order: messing up my mocks; messing up my apprenticeship; the triumph of my timber coming home; Mum's reaction to my pathetic exam results; her discovery of the garage; our awful argument.

I finish with a shrug. "I've failed at absolutely everything."

He's quiet for a long time, so long I think he's so disillusioned with me, he's lost for words.

Finally, he shakes his head. "You're just being pushed into the wrong shape, Nirvana."

I swallow. Am I the wrong shape for Jean-Louis too?

"Maybe," I tell him, "in part. But the other part is, I've been very lazy. I used to do quite well at school. I've just not tried hard enough."

"Perhaps, if you think so. But you're having to do too much on your own—work for your apprenticeship, work for school. If you have to try so hard, your school should help you. And your mother needs to recognise you have different skills."

He's right there, I think, and it should help to hear it put so clearly. Except it feels like he's expecting me to get my support from others now, not him anymore. Now he's fallen quiet again, and my gut tells me he's finally working up the courage to tell me. This is the end of our brief tangle in each other's lives. We helped each other for a while, hopefully his very worst while, but that's it for this magical, just-beginning thing we had. I know it.

I make my mind up. I'm going to get in there first. This is one thing I'm not going to bottle.

I look him in the eye. "I was reading Montaigne on the plane, Jean-Lou. The part on his friendship with de Boetie. And I want you to know, I think we could have that true friendship he writes about." I rush on before he can stop me. "I'd feel really lucky if we could continue to be friends."

His whole expression contorts.

"Just friends, you mean, Nirvana?"

"Well, it's not 'just', is it?" I say as fast as I can. "It's a huge thing. You're the only person in the world I can talk to about *every* thing."

He nods, but as he looks at me through our igloo light, his lips have tightened into a straight line.

"But you want the sort of friendship Montaigne and de Boetie shared?"

I look down, my stomach all jittery. "You don't?"

"No," he says, "I don't."

Not even that? Bracing myself, I drag my eyes back to him. He's shifted so he's kneeling up now, sideways on. I force myself to swivel more towards him, to face him.

Now *he's* trying to find the right words, I chew my cheek, determined not to cry.

"Forgive me, Nirvana."

I force myself not to look down, not to clap my hands over my ears to block out his apology of how this can't work, how sorry he is to have hurt me.

"I've made such a mess of this last week, cutting myself off from you."

I shake my head a little. If he's struggling to tell me the worst, I'm going to have to push him for the truth. "When *would* you have contacted me? If I had not come?"

"After collège today, honestly. I just needed a little time to process what had happened with Ghislaine. And I thought you knew, what we have, you and me, it's...rare."

The tautness inside me start to ease.

"I thought you were so...secure," he continues, "that you knew how I feel for you wasn't going to change suddenly or soon."

I relax a little further.

He bites his lip. "But I see now, I've been... unacceptable. From now on, I'll never go quiet on you, Nirvana, if you'll trust me again."

I catch my breath. *From now on.* I *do* believe him. I'm just not sure I can go through heartache like this again because he'll meet someone else eventually. Of course he will. I look him in the eye.

"But, Jean-Lou, you want someone who lives nearer, maybe from collège, someone cleverer and—"

"This isn't about your exams, is it, Nirvana?" he interrupts. "You know I don't care about things like that, except if it makes it harder for you to do what you want."

"Someone more...interesting then," I suggest.

"Than a *druide*?!" he says, his dimple appearing for the first time. "I hadn't met this someone who interested me even a little, Nirvana, till you appeared in my igloo!"

I open my mouth to point out I was there first, but his fingers are gentle on my cheek.

"Because you're everything I want," he whispers. "If that's all right with you?"

Is that all right with me?!

All but humming with happiness, I somehow scramble onto his lap, as close as I can get, my legs and arms wrapped tightly around him. He drops his head onto my shoulder again. Feeling again his defeat, sadness over his mum, I kiss the soft back of his neck, smooth his hair, shoulders, back, trying to ease it out of him, if I can.

Finally, he lifts his head and we share this no-holds-barred, cloudless-sky, full-sunshine of a beam. When our smiles allow us, we share a kiss too, telling each other...

You're all I want.

FIVE

"Tıme to go?" he asks, eventually.

We're both wearing jeans, totally useless as igloo wear! And we're hungry.

As we walk down the forest track, swinging our hands between us, I feel my being become lighter, for him and for me.

At the crossroads of the forest with Toblerone Wood, Jean-Lou introduces me to a mountain I've not been able to see before, beyond the wide field—La Crête des Bises. Above its sheer cliff face, its summit is bathed in an aura of golden sun.

I glance up at Jean-Lou. He beams at me. "I can't believe you're here, Nirvana," he says, dropping my hand to wrap his arm around my waist. I burrow into him.

Then I remember. "I need to text home now I'm with you."

"Where do your parents think you are?"

"Anywhere but here," I tell him, getting out my phone and turning it back on. "I'll have to tell them about you now, Jean-Lou."

"Of course."

But how, when they don't even know he exists?

Warily, I tug my phone out of my jeans and switch it back on. The screen's immediately jammed with notifications.

Missed Calls: twelve
WhatsApps: seven
Texts: six
Emails: two

All of them are from Mum, of course. I flash my screen at Jean-Lou, who grimaces. I don't even read them but open our family WhatsApp group and take a deep breath.

> NIV: I'm okay. I'm really sorry to have had
> my phone off. But I had to get back to Ouzon.
> I'm with a friend, Jean-Louis, who I met
> on the slopes and is the son of Monsieur
> Jaboulay from the resto. Will book flight
> home very soon.

I send Sab a quick message too to explain why I'm not at school, while Jean-Lou thumbs a message to update his dad on…me.

Then I turn my phone off again. Mum's answer is for later. First, we need our time.

"I know it's easy to say," he says, as we walk through Toblerone Wood, "but I think something good will come of you coming here. With your mum, I mean."

Really? Usually, I rate his judgement!

233

He's nodding, trying to convince me. "I was thinking in our igloo, you've been having to keep far too many secrets, trying to do things without the support of your family. Something had to change, and now it will."

I stop and turn to him in the middle of the woods, smiling. "It will, won't it?"

My running away here, I'd seen as another disaster, another failure notched up. But Jean-Lou's right: it's been a massive strain trying to hide everything. Mum's going to be even more furious with me now, and I'm going to have to face that when I get back. It's like a storm's been building for months, ever since I started sneaking to the Grove, skipping school on occasion. The pressure's risen and risen. Now the storm's broken, it can only bring some relief.

Back at the resto, Jean-Lou leads me up to their flat for the first time.

At the top of the steps, he hesitates on the little landing in front of the closed pine door.

"Only your dad's there, Jean-Lou," I say, standing beside him. Not her. Not anymore.

He nods and pushes the door.

IT OPENS INTO a short hallway then a living room. It's neither messy nor tidy, but has this unbalanced appearance, where his mother has removed her stuff and left odd gaps behind.

Jean-Lou leads us straight through it onto the little pine balcony at the end of the flat, as if he needs to get out again.

His dad appears behind us from one of the doors off the living room, brushing his hands.

"Nirvana, my dad, Gilbert," Jean-Lou says even though we've met before. His arm is around my shoulder. "This is Nirvana," he says needlessly, but I'm so glad he did because of the obvious pride in his voice.

His dad, who's no longer as forlorn, does a three-cheek-kiss move on me. I beam at him, this man who's helped shape Jean-Louis into the lad he is.

"You've lost your moustache!" I say, and he laughs, remembering Claude's false one. Jean-Lou looks mystified but smiles—at us having some history, I suppose.

"*Now* he's happy!" Gilbert says as he looks between us both.

Leaning in to Jean-Lou, I look up at him, thrilled that I at least got this right, can make so much difference to him that he's bounced back to his usual self from the crumbling lad I found an hour or so ago. In turn, he's given *me* back some hope in myself and my future.

"How's that little brother of yours?" Gilbert asks.

SITTING AT A table with Jean-Lou back down in the resto, while his dad's making some breakfast for all of us in the kitchen, I force myself to turn my phone back on.

> MUM: *Stay put, Nirvana. Arriving Ouzon around 5 p.m. tomorrow, Wednesday. I will sort our flights back.*

I tell Jean-Lou, my pulse pounding. Slowly, I try to explain how she's making me feel like a stupid kid who can't even be trusted to make her way home.

"You're not," he says simply. "We're both young. What we're doing, in trying to be together, is, I suppose... unusual. But we're not stupid."

I smile at him including himself in this, but my mouth's dry already at the prospect of tomorrow's trial.

"All the time and expense, the fuss of having Claude looked after, Mum'll be more fuming than ever," I warn him.

He reaches for my hand. "I'll be with you. And at least now she will meet me."

I nod, trying to see some good outcome from this rescue operation.

Now we know what time we have left, we make a plan. A Montaigne *when we're together we're together, make the most of every moment* plan: facing the music, that's tomorrow.

Then I reply to Mum, including telling her I won't have a signal for a while, send another message to Sab, telling her I'll be back at school on Thursday. *School.* What's Mum told them? I wonder. And how will I ever catch up now?

OVER THIS MOST delicious rösti dish—bacon, onions, potato and cheese—we tell his dad about Mum coming and what we'd like to do in our short time.

Like his son, Gilbert thinks about things before he reacts.

236

"So," he says, "you miss another day of collège? Sometimes other matters are more important."

If only Mum thought the same way.

"And try not to worry," he tells me, reading my expression. "I'll do what I can to help. I'd like to send your mother a message too, to let her know I'm here and know what you're doing."

I nod, surprisingly relieved to have his involvement, and give him Mum's number.

While we finish our food, he tells us he's decided to keep the resto closed until the February holidays to do some refurbishments inside—light pine all over to give it a whole new, bright look.

"Great idea, Papa," Jean-Lou tells him.

"What about giving it a new name too?" I blurt, then blush.

"I've never liked 'La Wetzet'," Jean-Lou tells me, wrinkling his nose. "It's some sort of ski move."

Gilbert looks at me. "Any ideas, Nirvana?"

I glance at Jean-Lou who nods his encouragement.

"How about 'L'Igloo'? A cosy place to shelter from bad weather."

Jean-Lou gives me a *I should have known!* nod.

"I like it!" Gilbert says.

"I've got some news too," Jean-Lou says.

We both look at him in surprise.

"Miska—you remember her, Nirvana?"

Of course I remember Marc's gorgeous husky!

"She's pregnant!"

Gilbert nods knowingly. "And you want one of her pups?"

Jean-Lou's eyes shine. "Is that all right, Papa?"

Now we're both looking at Gilbert.

"You've waited too long already to have a dog, Jean-Louis," he says. "When will the puppies be born?"

I gaze at Jean-Lou, made up for him.

"In about six weeks," he says.

I'm counting on from now in my head. That could fall around my half-term!

"Will I be able to come and see the puppy?" I blurt. Then I realise how presumptuous I've been.

"You're always welcome here, Nirvana," Gilbert says.

I can't stop smiling—at the new life both of them are already making and that I can be part of it, sometimes.

If Mum allows it.

If.

AFTER LUNCH, I retrieve my backpack and we go to Jean-Lou's bedroom. At the back of the building, it's only small with a tiny desk at an even tinier window. Not surprisingly, there are lots of books on the shelves over his bed, which is unmade, a few clothes on the floor. About the same level of messiness as my room, really.

I have a shower while he repacks a bag. While he showers, I lie on his bed, just for a minute. It smells of him, a warm mix of sleep and porridge somehow. Something cold and hard prods me in the neck. I reach under his pillow and smile when I find the *baguette magique.*

I open my eyes slowly. Jean-Lou's propped up against the wall at the other end of the bed, smiling at me.

"Better, Nirvana? You've been asleep for nearly two hours."

"Oh, no! Sorry! I slept at the airport last night."

He shakes his head a little. "That's okay," he says. "We still have daylight."

I stretch, think about sitting up, give up on it and smile back at him. "I wish you were always there when I woke up."

"Tomorrow morning, I will be again," he says, crawling up the quilt to hover over me, kiss me.

I tug him down. The more of his weight he gives me, the better I like it. We get lost for quite some time.

BEFORE WE SET off, Gilbert tells us he has had a reply from my mum: she and I will stay at the resto tomorrow night before leaving very early on Thursday morning.

"One last thing," he says as we're about to leave the resto. He pauses then flicks his eyes between us. "Be sensible!"

I look down at the floor, my cheeks scorching. I think we all know what he means we should be sensible about.

"Papa!" Jean-Lou murmurs, reproachful. "We know!"

We do. We sorted this out in his bedroom earlier. We know what's ab-so-lute-ly sensible for us. We also know it's not for now, not when his dad's taken responsibility for me but allowed us the freedom to have our night away.

Once we get to the bottom of the path, we stop and look at each other, smiling off our embarrassment.

"Sensible!" he says, his dimple deep, and bends to give me his most sensible-unsensible kiss till my tummy's like an upturned snow globe.

SIX

FROM HIS GRANDPARENTS' chalet, we can clearly see the tiny plateau which is home to our igloo. Here is where we've chosen to spend our one night. As soon as I step back inside, I feel the same wave of well-being I felt last time.

While Jean-Lou unpacks the all-important food in the little kitchen, I throw open the massively wide shutters. Then we stand at the window and watch the shifting pastel shades as the sun lowers itself gently behind la Pointe du Mont. I'm completely in these few minutes, with Jean-Lou, and completely content.

When most of the light has gone out of the sky, I turn and reach up to him. All of our kisses are unforgettable. But this, this is the happiest of all.

So far.

"If I could live anywhere in the world," I tell him, "it'd be here."

He gives me his beautiful smile.

"Then I'll share it with you, Nirvana, whenever you're here."

I smile back at him. If only!

"My grandmother left it to me in her will."

I pull in my bottom lip in excitement. "This is yours?"

He nods, but his face is serious now. "This is what caused the final argument with Ghislaine last week. She'd heard from the *immobilier* in Le Biot that they had a market for genuine Alpine chalets like this for good prices this year."

I shake my head, knowing what's coming.

He sniffs. "She wanted me to sell. To use the money to pay for university if I was insisting on going." He turns to me. "Papa finally saw how little she cared about me or understood what's important to him and me. This place is part of our family. Papa and I would hate to let it go."

"You won't, will you?" I say urgently. I couldn't bear to think of them without it.

"Never!" he says, smiling. "And we told her as much."

Finally, Jean-Lou turns on a lamp in the corner.

"There's electricity?" I say, amazed. "Last time, we had to use an oil lamp."

He gives me a sheepish look. "More ambience."

I put my hands on my hips, mock cross. "It made it much more difficult to see and measure the shepherd's table!" But actually, I'm delighted that he was thinking about creating a romantic atmosphere for us.

WHILE I LIGHT the fire and open up the shepherd's table, Jean-Lou prepares tea. It *feels* like his home. Maybe if I can play it right with Mum, we can be here together in summer, when the caramel-cream cows are on the high meadows, clanging their bells, and the sky holds its light till midnight.

Jean-Lou comes over to rest a tin of tartiflette from the resto in the flames to reheat then comes and sits with me at the shepherd's table, where I physically point to its various components, and he helps me draw up a day-by-day schedule that will ensure my miner's table is finished in time to send the final photographs with my application for Winslow Wood.

As we work through it, he checks with me exactly what's involved at each stage and whether I can realistically get it done in two hours a day—apart from weekends, when I obviously have much more time. For the tabletop, instead of pegging the boards together, I tell Jean-Lou I'll use cross-members underneath, which is far quicker. We even discuss the joints, which are the most time-consuming part, and I make the decision to drop the more complicated dovetails for simple half-lap corners.

Otherwise, we've already included two hours homework or tuition on each school night too.

We look at each other across the table.

"It's a lot," he says. "Can you do it?"

"It *is* a lot. But it is only for three weeks. Once the table is finished, I'll have even more time for schoolwork."

Once we're satisfied, we eat.

Sitting on the rug by the fire, we watch the flames. We play draughts on a wooden board, and I win best of five! Next, we invent a game where we take turns at naming a category and have to come up with our favourites on the count of three: food, colour, (same—green); animal (same—dog, of course!); drink; film; parts of each other's body (same—lips…so far!).

Music…it takes us a while to find something we like in common, but when we do, it's magic! Turns out our grandparents, all teenagers in the 1960s, have also passed down to us a love of the Beatles, so we make a list of our very favourite of their songs to play at our postponed all-night igloo party, whenever that might be. Jean-Lou understands more English than I thought, but I challenge him to understand *all* the lyrics by then, not just the first lines. Neither of us are dancers, but we reckon we could dance with each other, especially on the dance floor that will be the clearing outside our igloo.

Sometimes we chat about our adventure tomorrow. Often, we kiss, getting ahead, I think, to cover the time till we're next together, then it'll be catching up! But also, we just *are*...till my eyelids start to droop, and I fight it. I don't want this day to ever end.

We're not about to waste eight hours apart. The heat from the fire wafts through the open bedroom door. As I fantasised two weeks ago, we're together in his grandparents' bed, unused for decades as his mother refused to come here. My skin's on high alert as, in underwear and T-shirts, our bare legs interweave. Gradually, though, our bodies become more familiar and relax into each other. We don't kiss. If we start, they'll become lovers' kisses, skin will find more skin, and we'll slip into one syrup-smooth sequence our bodies—which know exactly what to do—won't want to stop. That's for another time. A time when we're prepared and won't be making things worse for ourselves. If there is such a time.

For now, I just watch the shadows of flickering flames on the pine wall.

"Look!" Jean-Lou says, once the glow from the fire dims and the shadows fall.

I wriggle around in his arms to face the window. We've left the shutters open too, and now the room's dark, we can see stars pinned all across the solid black of the night sky.

"Wouldn't it be fabulous?" I whisper, turning around to him eventually, "if we got snowed in for a week?"

"Sorry, Nirvana, the sky's too clear for snow."

"But it could change."

"Mmm," he says, sleepily.

"Jean-Lou..." I have to get this off my mind before I can sleep. "What if this is our last night ever together?"

"We won't allow it to be," he murmurs.

No, we really won't, I think, as he shuffles down to cushion his head on my chest. Remembering the Jean-Lou I first saw this morning, I stroke his hair till his hand grows heavy on my hipbone. Then I wrap my arm around his shoulders, shielding him from all further hurt.

This is why I came.

WHEN I WAKE, in the same position, threads of grey are beginning to lighten the darkness framed by the shutters. I gently extract myself from under Jean-Lou, who turns towards the wall, burying his head in the pillow.

All the heat's gone from the chalet when I get out of bed. I pull on my socks, jeans and hoodie and go to light the fire. As I stretch by the window, it's as Jean-Lou said, no new snow. But that's all right because soon we're off beyond the furthest mountains where first light is dawning.

SEVEN

W**E'RE LATE.**
       My stomach's all clenched up as we dash into
the resto, Jean-Lou having spotted what must be Mum's
hire car outside. I'm terrified—not at her wrath at the
'stunt' I've pulled but because everything for me and
Jean-Lou hinges on this meeting.

I stop in the archway to the dining area, overcome
with apprehension. They've not noticed us yet. Mum's
already sitting at a table in front of the bar with Gilbert,
a pot of tea between them. At least they're not complete
strangers. I look at Jean-Lou. This is hardly a bundle of
fun for him either. But he lifts his chin and takes my hand.

Tearing my eyes away from Jean-Lou's face, I take
a deep breath and we step towards our parents.

They both stand up. We drop hands.

Do I hug Mum or not? Wishing I'd planned this out
with Jean-Lou, I dither too long, and Gilbert jumps in.

"This is Jean-Louis," he tells her. "Jean-Louis, Madame
Green-Bertholet."

I hold my breath. Mum will soon see how amazing
Jean-Lou is!

"Stella," she says, holding out her hand to him.

"I'm very happy finally to meet you," he replies in
French, of course, shaking her hand.

"Hot chocolate, Nirvana?" Gilbert asks me.

I nod, smiling my thanks.

"Is Claude all right?" I ask Mum quickly in English. "Rova, Grandad?"

Her nod and blink say, *no thanks to you.*

My tummy tightens still further. With her hair tied back, her eyes are so obviously tired, strained.

"So sorry we were late, Mum," I tell her, as we sit down opposite her. I switch to French, for Jean-Lou's sake. "We were dependent on Marc, the friend of Jean-Louis, for our lift back."

"He was taking his husky dog team for a race in Chamonix," Jean-Lou adds, "so we went along."

"Towing a trailer of six howling, excited dogs behind us!" I tell Mum, in English. "Though they were so quiet they must have been asleep on the way back. And Mont Blanc was incredible *sans chapeau...*"

Unusually, and so lucky for us, you could see its head without its hat of clouds.

But I peter out then as I become aware she's looking down at the table. Our stolen day out isn't what she's come to hear about. I need to come down to earth, get real.

Gilbert appears with my chocolate and a coffee for Jean-Lou.

"I am making special pizza," he says. "It will be ready in half an hour or so, if that's all right."

We all nod. "Thanks so much, Gilbert," Mum says.

As we sip our drinks, an awkward silence lingers. Is Mum expecting Jean-Lou to leave us alone once he's finished his coffee? I don't want him to go. Without him, I'd be in the dock with no defence.

"So," she says in French, putting her clasped hands on the table in front of her. I brace myself. She's about to start her case for the prosecution. "How did you two come to meet?"

I clutch for Jean-Lou's hand between us. We'd be useless criminals, not having got our full story straight. How far do I go with the truth?

"Jean-Louis helped me when I fell off the lift-pull on the blue piste," I say, which is true but not the answer to her question.

How can I mention all the rest without making things a myriad times worse: how he introduced me to all the mountains on Christmas Eve night, the hike to his grandparents' chalet, the night we fell asleep?

Mum angles her head at me, waiting for more.

I swallow. "I might have... I *did* miss my ski lessons after that," I say in English.

She gives a little exasperated shake of her head.

I shrug. "We sheltered in an igloo."

"We talked about Ruskin and Montaigne," Jean-Lou chips in, picking up on 'igloo'.

Mum's eyes widen as she gives me an astonished look.

I glance at him sideways. *Don't mention the nights,* I urge him.

Mum sits back and looks at us both.

"It's a nice story."

But it is just a story is implied. My shoulders tense again as I await her next move.

"I've been hearing from your father, Jean-Louis, how well you are doing at college. Your expected BAC scores are very high. And you could study philosophy at one of the best universities?"

It goes quiet. This isn't an innocent compliment. My stomach sickens at the implication that unlike Mum, his father has nothing to worry about. Jean-Lou's shuffling tells me he's not comfortable either.

"That's because I'm naturally interested in philosophy," he tells her. "It's my passion. I'm not trying to be successful. I might equally decide…" he shoots me a quick look, "to stay in the mountains, help Papa with the resto and do my own philosophising."

I shoot him a look back. This is news to me! Or is he just making a point?

Mum's face is puzzled, as if he's speaking a different language and not just French! Our thinking is out of kilter with hers, but I love how Jean-Lou speaks as an equal to her.

"Nirvana," Mum says, bumping her hands on the table as she gets back to her point, "she's very young, only just sixteen."

I am actually here, you know!

"She's also been struggling at school recently."

Thanks, Mum! That's the last joy of the day slapped out of me.

Miserable, I look down at the table. Jean-Lou doesn't need this implication of guilt laid on him. Nor can I come up with any counter-argument when those are the facts.

"I have my own passion too," I tell her, scrambling in my backpack. "Look," I say in English, laying my sheet of paper on the table, facing her, only it's really crumpled now. "We've made a timetable. For every day, we have put in my homework or revision time, and the time to build the table. It's going to be my own adaptation of a shepherd's table, like Jean-Louis' grandparents used to have."

I reach for my phone to show her a photo of it, but she's hardly even glancing at our schedule, so I just lay my phone on the table.

"Nirvana" she replies, also in English, "you've been having a lovely time, but during two days of absence from school, which would have been unauthorised had I not given the reason of 'family difficulties'. You've got to live in the real world…"

I swallow and shut my eyes against a patronising phrase I loathe. *My world's been real enough, hard enough,* I want to tell her.

"You need qualifications and skills. You have to be able to support yourself. As we have just found out, you need to focus on school now, not be distracted by someone hundreds of miles away."

She spreads her hands as if that's it, all there is to say. End of Jean-Lou. But I haven't had my say yet, and I *won't* give him up.

Lost in the English, Jean-Lou reaches for my hand on the table. "Nirvana," he says in a low voice, "do you want me to stay or leave you to talk with your mother?"

I glance at Mum and long to tell him not to leave me. Once he's gone, not only will Mum's version of me prevail, but worse, of *us* too. A version that turns the two of us into another of my many mess-ups.

"You'd better go help your dad," I tell him instead, wretched as I sense defeat.

He covers my hand with his for a moment, warming it, then leaves me.

MUM SOFTENS SLIGHTLY. "He's a grand young man."

"He is, isn't he?" I beam, so proud of him. "He—"

But she holds up her hand. *Enough of him; this is about you.*

"He, his father, they are charming, but completely unrealistic. Do you have any idea of the gravity of what you've done, Nirvana?"

I steel myself. *The time of reckoning.*

"We were so frightened when your room was empty, your passport gone. A young girl on your own. It was so…reckless, and so very immature, Niv."

I look down at the table: I was so caught up in myself, I didn't think of the effect on my family, not properly. What will Claude have thought? And my Grandad?

"I need to know that you realise the seriousness of this absconding, Nirvana."

Absconding? That's what you do from prison, isn't it? At the same time, I can't deny her side of the story, of what I've done.

"I do realise," I say, looking her in the eye now. "And I'm sorry, truly I am, Mum. I genuinely didn't want to put you through all this. And I'm really, *really* sorry about using your card and money."

Thing is, though, I'd do it all again.

She studies me across the table, almost as if she can tell what I'm thinking.

250

"What also flabbergasts me, Nirvana, is this whole secret life you've had going on here as well as at home— the deceit of it, long-term. I'd never have thought it of you."

My mouth turns down. "I've *hated* it, Mum. I never wanted to hide things from you all. But it was the only way I could do the things I wanted."

She heaves an exasperated sigh. "None of us get to do what we want all the time, Niv."

"No, but I can't even have the things that mean most to me—unless in secret."

"Ah," she says, knowingly, "we're back to Jean-Louis."

"Thing is, Mum," I tell her, "this, me coming here, isn't only about him."

She raises her eyebrows at me, as if to say, *Look where we are.*

And then he appears between us, with a glass of red wine for Mum and fizzy water for me.

"Sorry to interrupt, but Papa asked if you're ready to eat in five minutes?"

I glance at Mum. In spite of it all, I'm starving.

"Yes, and thanks a lot, Jean-Louis," she says.

I gaze at her over her long slurp of wine.

The judge adjourns for tea.

But of course, we already know the verdict.

EIGHT

"T HAT IS AMAZING, thank you," I tell Gilbert across the huge, steaming pizza between us, with ham, mushrooms and Reblochon cheese. It's exactly what we need after our freezing day.

It falls quiet as we all start eating.

"Until today," Jean-Lou suddenly says, taking me by surprise as he's speaking to Mum, "I'd never seen Mont Blanc close up. It was a great opportunity when I heard Nirvana had also wanted to see it for ages."

Mum looks wide-eyed at me as she chews, and I start to suspect Jean-Lou has picked up on what she was saying about missing school earlier and is maybe giving me the chance to show today's experience has been part of my education too.

"We studied Ruskin's paintings of Mont Blanc in art," I tell her, "so it was brilliant to see the glaciers in reality."

The French I'm speaking for Jean-Lou and his dad's sake feels totally fake between Mum and me.

"You know you view Mont Blanc from the peak next to it?" I check with Mum, in English. "The Aiguille du Midi." As its name says, the sharp needle of a mountain. She shakes her head through her mouthful. "It's so high, it takes twenty minutes to get up even in a lift. Then it was absolutely freezing out on the viewing platform."

I find the best photo on my phone and hold it out to her. She actually looks and nods.

"You've been very kind to take Nirvana," she tells Jean-Lou, making me sound like a child—and like it was a last treat too.

He shakes his head a little as she gets it—him—wrong again. My Jean-Lou who told me the night we met I'd see Mont Blanc one day.

"We even got to see the end of the husky race back down in the valley!" I tell Gilbert.

He smiles. "How did Marc's team do?"

"The dogs are still young," Jean-Lou says, "so as well as he'd hoped."

I glance at Mum and wonder if I'll ever be able to tell her about how they pulled us way up la Pointe du Mont a couple of weeks ago.

"Jean-Louis's going to have a pup from one of the dogs on the team," I tell Mum.

She just nods. This holding back of enthusiasm and feelings, it's about not giving me any hope of getting involved in life here.

Gilbert pours Mum and himself another glass of wine while Jean-Lou offers more pizza around.

Mum leans back in her chair and looks around the room as she sips it. "So, what are your plans for the resto, Gilbert?"

He half turns in his seat. "This whole end, a huge window," he says, indicating behind him, where we can only see parts of the piste and mountains now. Then," he twists back around, "to re-clad all the walls in new, light pine." He turns back to the table. "And Nirvana has given it a new name. L'Igloo."

Even Mum smiles at that.

She can see, can't she, I fit here? With Jean-Lou. I really do!

NOW EVERYONE'S FINISHED eating, he and I start to gather up the dishes to take into the kitchen.

"How's it going?" he asks as he stacks the plates in the big dishwasher.

I lean back against the counter. "Much better when you and your dad are there." I look at him, my mouth turning down. "She still doesn't understand me. On my own, I just seem…ridiculous."

"You're not, I promise you. Just be yourself."

"But that's the whole problem, isn't it?"

He shakes his head, smiling. "You're *vife*, Nirvana."

I watch his lips as he stresses *vife*, like the highest possible compliment it is—one French word summing up several English adjectives: alive, intelligent, radiant. All the ways I see him too. Now I smile at him.

Resting gently into me, he gives me his sweetest, most focused kiss.

You're just right the way you are, Nirvana.

"Oh!" a voice says behind him. Mum's.

We pull apart.

She puts the platters down and leaves again.

I look at Jean-Lou, biting my lip.

"S'okay," he says, shrugging. "This is us."

Yeah, but she has our future in her hands.

"THANK YOU SO much for such a delicious meal," Mum tells Gilbert, after we've finished this light, frothy afters called *Îles flottantes* because wispy islands of meringue float on an eggy-creamy sea. "The least I can do is clear up."

Gilbert won't hear of it.

Mum looks at me. "Shall we go for a walk then, Niv?" I hesitate: don't want to spend even a minute of our last night away from Jean-Lou. We'd planned to go to our igloo, but Mum wasn't asking a question. And anyway, somehow, God knows how, before we leave early tomorrow morning, I've got to convince her to let me keep seeing Jean-Lou.

"Take a torch, Nirvana," Jean-Lou says, going behind the bar to get his from the flat.

I follow him up.

"I don't want to leave you," I tell him, burying my head in his shoulder.

I mean this walk now, but also tomorrow and every day after that. And he knows it. He holds me close and safe, stroking my hair.

"Don't give up," he whispers to me. "Explain how it feels."

I nod. He gives me a fortifying kiss then hands me his big yellow torch.

NINE

As I step out of the warm bath that's being with Jean-Lou, into the bitingly clear night, everything in me wants to turn straight around and go back to him. But Mum's pointing up and away from the resto.

"While we talk," she says, "let's find out what's through that little wood."

She means Toblerone Wood. *Our* wood.

We march fast to keep warm to start with, so fast we can't, or don't, talk, down the car park, across the bottom of the piste and up the slope towards the wood. With each step away from the resto, my every atom is pulled harder back to Jean-Lou.

So few hours left with him. *Ever*, maybe.

As we reach the edge of the trees, Mum stops. "Niv, you were saying before tea, you coming here wasn't only about Jean-Louis. What was it then?"

Explain how you feel, Jean-Lou's voice says in my head.

You can do it, the pines tell me.

I light our way between the trees and walk forward.

"I was…desperate. At a loss."

"Your exam results?"

"Yes, I s'pose."

Though not only. *Of course* coming here was also about Jean-Lou. And my apprenticeship too.

"I've found GCSE work a lot harder than you realised, Mum. Well, at least till this week!"

She gives a hollow sort of laugh at the meeting between her, Dominique and me that sparked this whole thing.

"That's because you've been distracted," she tells me, putting my back up all over again. "Grandad's timber. What *has* been going on with that?"

There's nothing for it now but the truth about Alz bringing the wood to the Grove in September for me to work on.

"Good grief, Niv!" she says. "Those woods are so dangerous! You've taken such risks, then and now."

I lick my lips. "How else can I do the things I want, Mum, when you'd banned Hackspace?"

Would never have let me come and see Jean-Louis.

"But we were right to, weren't we, given your results?"

"No!" I say. We're getting close the far end of our little wood now. "It's not as simple as that. It's not about lack of time. I can sit in my room all the hours of the day trying to study, but it won't mean I do better."

She stops us. "Then what will?"

I look at her through the torch's beam and shrug a bit. "I need some help. I've got lost, left behind, and no one's noticed." Or cared. "But I admit, I've also let things slide. I could have asked for that help, and…my thinking's lazy when I'm not interested."

Even in the limited light, I can make out one of those *and there you have it* looks. My lack of interest is the root cause. Back to me again. I sigh. Maybe it is.

Explain how it feels.

"Because," I start us walking again, towards the natural light, the moonlight, "I'm being forced into the wrong hole."

The image is so clear in my head of Claude as a toddler, trying to jam a square into a triangular slot in his shape sorter. Spatial stuff was one of the few things he wasn't good at. It's pretty painful when it's *me* being shoved around though!

"You mean exams again?"

"Not only. Other things—from ski lessons to A' levels. I've thought about what Dominique said that time in the chalet, about doing A' levels if you can. And maybe I could. Maybe I could manage French, art and something else, as you suggested. But even those subjects I like would make me unhappy. It's like...like if *you* were made to spend two years of your life making furniture!"

Though even A' levels would be nothing compared to not seeing Jean-Louis again, I want to add.

Mum huffs out a long sigh. "But we all have to fit into some framework, to show we're equipped for the job we want to do. Exams are an important part of the world we live in. It can't all be about happiness."

Then it's an imperfect world, I think, *with stupid tests and hurdles all over the place.*

"And as your parents," she goes on, "we have to guide you through these milestones in your life. Because they determine *your* future."

My shoulders drop. "I know that now, Mum."

I know if I don't 'prove' myself through GCSEs, I can't access my right place in this world I *am* a part of. So I tell Mum how I've sabotaged my apprenticeship chances by not taking science seriously enough. And I admit I needed to be more orderly and disciplined about my woodwork. The chaotic state of the garage gave a really bad impression, when really the table is all clear in my mind.

As we emerge from the trees, the Moon has decided to join us, warming the vast white meadow that falls away before us. Beyond it, stands La Crète des Bises, craggy yet kindly in the moonlight.

"Stunning!" Mum exclaims, sweeping a hand back to Toblerone Wood, forward and up towards the mountains. "I never saw this when we were here."

You were too busy zooming around on metal, I think.

We stand and bask in this nighttime beauty.

Then Mum turns to me. "What *do* you want, Niv?" she asks, softly.

Finally.

My eyes are drawn up to the Crète.

Be strong, they murmur down to me. *Be proud.*

I look Mum in the eye.

So little and so much, all at the same time.

"To be me."

"Is THIS AS far as we go?" she asks, after a long moment.

It has to be, I think as I gaze back into Toblerone Wood, magnetised towards Jean-Lou, my minutes with him trickling away like sand through my fingers. The only other way to go is up the dark, steep track to our right. While it's something, really something that Mum's finally asked what *I* want, I'm never more myself than when

I'm with Jean-Lou. More than anything, I *must*, go on seeing him.

But does she get that?

Maybe if I invest a bit more of mine and Jean-Lou's now-time, I can win us lots of future times.

"We can go a little further," I tell her.

I switch the torch back on and point it uphill, to the path that intersects the deep forest and leads to our igloo.

Eventually, I stop us and direct the beam towards the half of the trees on our left. By scanning the light around, I find our tracks, mine and Jean-Lou's, from yesterday since it's not snowed since.

"Our igloo's along there," I tell Mum. "Our second one." I tell her about Ghislaine having our first igloo destroyed.

"When you asked about mothers not loving their children, you were really asking me about Jean-Louis, Niv, weren't you?" she asks rhetorically. "Gilbert has told me about Jean-Louis' mother. He's clearly thrived, though, thanks to his dad."

"He has!" I'm...heartened she's talking about him in this positive way. "But that doesn't mean it hasn't hurt him though," I say, defensive now. "Including an awful week with her before she finally went. Jean-Louis was struggling yesterday." He needs *me* as well as his dad, I want to add.

"Do you...would you let me see your igloo, Niv? I've never seen a real one."

NO! Everything in me objects. *It's our refuge, Jean-Lou's and mine. No one else has ever seen it.* But as we stand in this cold, clear night among the wise, listening trees, instead of blurting out the first thing that comes into my head, I think it through. And I wonder, *What's Mum really after in asking to see our igloo?*

Directing the light so we can both see it, I lead our way into the forest, the first boundary between the outside world and Jean-Lou's and mine.

The fallen tree, a second threshold, gives me an excuse. I could lie and say I've lost our way, that we'd better turn back now. She wouldn't know otherwise. That'd get me back to Jean-Lou quicker. But we need more than tonight. So I clamber over it, turning to light the way for Mum.

It's darker from there on, deeper into the forest, but at least now we can follow the little fan of light side by side.

The trees start to thin out as we get nearer our clearing. And suddenly, we're there.

Mum gasps.

OUR IGLOO IS in the full spotlight of the Moon. No need for a torch here! My heart gives a violent lurch of objection that I'm here without Jean-Lou.

"How lovely!" Mum whispers.

She walks all the way around it while I wait at the edge of the clearing, our first kiss just outside our igloo entrance so vivid in my head.

"It's perfectly built, Niv," Mum says, cutting into my thoughts, "like one you see in drawings. And *you* did it!"

"Me and Jean-Louis. But yeah, that's what Ruskin said about building anything. You create it for use, but also it needs to be beautiful."

I wanted all that for Jean-Lou when we built this—both for while I was with him and when he was on his own here.

"That's also what I'm trying—*was* trying to do," I correct myself, "with Grandad's table. The thinking is, I put something of myself into it so Grandad feels the connection with me as well as his tree every time he uses it."

"When did you get to be such a philosopher, Niv?" Mum asks, teasing a little.

"I think I always was," I say.

"May I look inside?" she asks.

That mangles my heart all over again.

TEN

"YOU CAN LOOK," I manage, eventually. But no more.

I step towards her and give her the torch.

She crouches down then pokes her head just into the entrance, casting the beam all around the dome. I can see it glowing from the outside.

She tips forward. *No! Stop!* is on my lips. *You can't go in!*

That really would be trespassing.

But she stops, reverses right out and straightens up again.

"Thank you for showing me," she says quietly as we stand just outside the entrance of our igloo. She hands the torch back to me. "You've been having to hide yourself away, haven't you, Niv love?"

Everything stills.

I can't speak.

Clutching the light, I step away from her, around the side of our igloo, mindlessly skimming my hand over the curves of its roof as I walk to its other end.

She sighs. "Thinking of you having to find refuge in an igloo, deep in a forest, it brings back how it felt to have to hide the truth from my own parents."

It's the very last thing I expected her to say! I keep quiet, waiting for more.

263

"I think your grandad would agree, it was hard on all of us when I first told them I was gay."

"Really, Mum?" I screw up my eyes for a second. "Nana and he always seemed totally cool with it."

And she and Grandad are as close as two fingers now! Close in a different way from him and me.

"Eventually, yes," she says. "But it took time. You took me totally by surprise when you told me about your apprenticeship on Boxing Day, so near to the deadline too. I said things on the spur of the moment I shouldn't have, Niv."

I shrug. "Not if that's what you thought."

"I'm finding I'm having to rethink lots of things just now," she says. "Just like with my parents, my daughter taking a different direction than I thought, it needs a lot of explaining and a lot of listening."

At this first hint of hope, my heart warms—the only warm bit of me!

"Maybe that's where we've both gone wrong, Niv. I should have listened, much, much more closely."

I find myself smiling, just a little, for the first time since we came out. "I do keep a lot of my thinking to myself, I know, Mum."

"And I seem to have lost the knack of knowing as you've got older!" She smiles back at me across the length of the igloo. "So, I needed you to tell me, love, about getting behind in some subjects, about wanting to make furniture for Grandad from our very own tree. You named him Querky, but he was an important part of my childhood too."

Caught up in my own feelings, I've overlooked so much as well, I have to admit. Not only did Mum lose her mum, but Querky and her childhood home too. While my heart hurts for her for the first time in ages, I also like that link between us. But I do need her to understand why I couldn't tell her about the wood from our oak.

"It was the risk," I explain, "that if I told you about the timber, about Jean-Louis, you'd say no, just like you did about Hackspace. Cos ever since the council killed Querky, despite all we did to try to protect him, the things I love the most have been taken away from me."

Mum's face is crumpling, but she's asked me to say what's in my head so I go on.

"I've felt adults…block what I want. The council. School wouldn't let me do both art and DT for GCSE and also…"

I hesitate.

"Also me, you mean. Of course you do." Mum's voice is small in the clearing. "For your own mother to be taking away the things you care about…"

The sad shakes of her head make my heart twinge again. But one last truth is buzzing around my head, looking for an outlet.

"I *have* felt that I don't…fit in the family anymore."

Apart from with Rova. Even with Grandad, I've had to keep the same secrets.

Mum's listening at last. So I keep going, opening up, explaining.

"It's helped, really helped, meeting Jean-Louis because I *totally* fit with him. But, even though I've never been that bothered before, I've started to think more and more about my donor dad. That maybe my practical side comes from him and *he'd* get it."

With a wince, she closes her eyes for a moment. We haven't talked about my father, whoever he may be, since THE TALK with Claude a couple of years ago brought it up again for me too.

"We've always talked about you finding out more about your donor—your donor dad," Mum corrects herself, "now you're sixteen and when you're ready, Niv. But I wanted it to be for *positive* reasons, not that you felt *pushed* towards him because you don't feel...at home in your own family. Well, I've let you down." Her voice is all thin and sorrowful. "When I thought we were such a close, happy family."

Oh! "We are, Mum!"

She shakes her head. "That doesn't fit with what you've been telling me, Niv."

I step towards her, down the igloo's side. "We *do* have happy times, Mum, I promise you! Even though I had secrets going on, I loved it here in the chalet. At home, I love our family times, mad teas when Grandad comes round, the board games and all Claude's craziness! And we have really deep roots that keep us going, Mum. I had the most amazingly happy childhood. It's just...I'm not a child anymore. And not everything that worked in your life works in mine. But we don't have to be the same to be close. Just look at you and Grandad."

Or me and Jean-Lou.

Jean-Lou.

Mum and me, we've come a long way tonight, but what about him? I'm about to explain to my new listening mother how much we need to see each other, but she speaks first.

"Show me what this special table would look like."

I dig out my phone and scroll down as I slowly move towards her.

Holding the image of the shepherd's table in front of her, I explain how mine would be different—bespoke, for my Grandad.

"That's incredibly thoughtful, Niv," she says, as I pocket my phone again. "I've never seen anything like it. From his precious tree too! And you can actually build this?"

"It's a lot to do in the time, but yeah. And I hoped it'd really stand out in my apprenticeship application."

"This isn't just a fad, is it? I can tell that now. Your heart's really set on it."

I heave a sigh. "It was. My science isn't up to it, though."

"Then we need to get you a support team. You said how everything felt like scaling Mont Blanc to you. Well, nobody does that on their own, do they? They're all roped up, helping each other out, and they have the right equipment. You need the right tools. Grandad's giving us some money from the sale of Oak Vista—"

I reach out and hug her, re-remembering her softness. This is like it used to be between us—Mum finding a way through for me instead of throwing up obstacles I have to take massive and secret detours around. This is her *enabling* me to be me!

"I'm so, so glad you got to see our igloo," I tell her, sharing my positive thoughts too.

Infinitely more importantly, though, I'm glad that you've finally met Jean-Lou.

Now's my moment, now Mum's finally recognised the real me.

"I don't know about you, Niv," she's saying, "but I'm beginning to freeze."

She steps towards the edge of the clearing, but my feet won't move and my breathing's a bit panicky. I'm about to leave behind our igloo, probably forever.

"What is it, love?" Mum asks, turning back. "You're trembling."

I can't speak, and the fact that she even has to ask tells me she hasn't really listened—not to everything. I said how I've found my fit with Jean-Louis. All tonight's talking, brilliant though it's been, will count as nothing if she tries to take him away from me.

"It's Jean-Louis, isn't it?" she says gently.

A sort of squeak emerges from me. "I will see him after tonight."

I mean it as a statement, but my voice, my tone, isn't strong enough, and it comes out as more of a question. If I can't, all the bridges we've tentatively rebuilt tonight will collapse.

She looks straight out in front of her, wipes a hand over her mouth. "This is..." She shakes her head.

My hopes shrink into a tiny, anguished ball.

"It's so hard. He's a lovely lad—very caring, protective of you."

I'm waiting for the 'but'.

"But honestly Niv, love, how *can* you continue to see each other?"

"He can come and stay at half-term. Then I'd come here at Easter," I say, trying to hold her gaze; trying to make it sound perfectly reasonable.

My mind previews images of the whole summer here, staying up at Chalet Ouzon, helping at the resto, swimming naked together in mountain lakes…

"I *am* listening, love…" she says. "I am, but your apprenticeship is going to take all your focus, isn't it?"

A watery boom starts up again in my head.

"And I know you won't want to hear this," she goes on, "but however real this feeling is now, it *is* just a first crush for you both—"

"It's not!" I break in. "It's much more than that. It's real—a real friendship, Mum. We think in the same way about things, about life."

She sighs a little into the night. "It's not just friendship, though, is it? That'd be far simpler. You're pretty… physical with each other." *You don't know the half of it,* I think. "Someday, it'll have to end in tears. And it'll be more painful the longer you manage to keep it going."

"I don't know about our future, Mum, but we can't be ripped apart. Just can't."

I know from her face, the taut body language, that she's far from convinced.

"He *totally* gets me. And wants the best for me too. He's very supportive."

She looks at me through the yellow light. "I can see that. I don't doubt how… good he would be for you…"

My hopes, which had started to rise, fall again at the 'would'.

269

JENNIFER BURKINSHAW

"If you lived near each other. But your life's in
Lancashire, love, not here." Her voice is gentle but the
meaning isn't. "You and Jean-Louis, especially at the ages
you are...a long-distance relationship when you've only
just met. Can *you* see it working?"

I want to clamp my hands over my ears and block out
all her objections. I know it *looks* like it'd be really hard.
I just know we have to try.

Because he's
the easiest
clearest
brightest
part of my life.

But I can't say that to Mum without being offensive.

"Isn't that up to us?" I say instead. "It's all part of
you letting me be independent, make my own decisions
about what's right for me. It's every bit as much about
Jean-Louis as my apprenticeship."

She looks back towards the igloo. Back to me.

"Yes. Yes, I suppose so. You've grown up in ways
I've not noticed, Niv. And Jean-Louis has had to, too."
She hesitates again. "Over to you then. I know the two of
you will make the right decision."

270

ELEVEN

As I LEAD the way back to the fallen tree, a light appears, moving towards us. It can only be Jean-Lou.

"I thought you must be here," he says, taking us in. He strides over the trunk straight to me, spreading his arm around my shoulder. "Okay?"

"We have been quite a time, haven't we?" Mum says.

"I've brought some hot chocolate," he says, holding up a flask.

"You two share it," she says, "in your igloo. Just lend me that torch, Niv."

"Are you sure you know the way back?" Jean-Lou checks.

"I'll follow your tracks."

"YOU'RE SHAKING," JEAN-LOU says, turning to me once Mum is on her way. He shoves the flask back into his pocket and unzips his jacket to share his body heat with me. I wriggle myself into him. "Was it so bad... with your mum?"

I pause. I don't want to be thoughtless here. The contrast between our mothers is starker than ever now my mum has done a U-turn, is supporting who and what I want to be.

"It was good," I tell him quietly. "I'm just so cold."

"You didn't think to go in our igloo?" he asks, rubbing my back and shoulders.

I shake my head hard. "That's only for us."

In our igloo, with my hands wrapped around the metal cup from the flask, I try to sum up everything Mum and I talked about, the new-old understanding we found and good news about my apprenticeship.

I look him in the eyes as we sit facing each other, cross-legged. "Then she said she's leaving it to us—whether we try to keep…going."

I know full well, when she talked about us the doing the right thing, her thinking was if she didn't force a decision on us, we'd realise for ourselves our relationship was impossible.

"But we'll only see each other a few times a year," I add quietly.

He gazes back at me through our soft igloo light. "We've always known that really, haven't we?"

I nod, chewing my lip. "And she says it can only end… badly."

We both go quiet for a loooong time. Literally minutes. During those minutes, I'm trying to think what's best for him, and I know he's doing the same for me.

We're probably as good as it gets in terms of mindfulness, but it still hurts to be away from each other. If we stop now, it will already rip my heart apart. And his. But isn't that going to happen anyway eventually? Only far, far more badly, though that's hard to imagine. At sixteen and seventeen, with me doing an apprenticeship a thousand miles away from him studying at uni—or even working in the resto—*if* we even get that far—you don't need to be good at maths to figure out the odds of that working as we both start on new paths.

We've fallen hard, fast and deep for each other and, I know now, equally. Maybe because it is the first time for both of us, as Mum said, who knows? Are we storing up inevitable and ever-increasing anguish for each other the longer we go on?

Maybe we do quit while everything's sweet and perfect between us—like our igloo, before it disintegrates under the warmth of spring. Before we get bored or irritated with each other or one of us wants to stop and not the other and our glorious memories are tainted and soured.

"What're you thinking, Nirvana?" he says after a while.

I exhale all my thoughts. Our igloo is a place only for truth.

"Loads of things. It feels different to be given the decision. Not in the sense that we're no longer a secret..." The forbidden part of it was a necessity for us, not a driver. "But because, finally, we have control."

He nods. "And with control comes responsibility."

I trust his instinct. Part of that responsibility towards each other is a huge, overwhelming protectiveness too. It's *because* of how strongly we feel for each other that we're making the decision we are.

A loud rushing like a huge waterfall sets off in my head. Tilting forward, seeing each other only through a sheen of tears, we share our goodbye kiss.

EPILOGUE:
31 JANUARY

EPILOGUE:
31 JANUARY

THE MINER'S TABLE is at ninety degrees to the garage side entrance, its back towards the main shutter door, to give it maximum space in front and around it. It's toasty warm in here because I've had the electric heater on all morning.

"Er, I've...I've been making something, Grandad," I tell him, precise words escaping me now the big moment's come.

"Right," he says uncertainly, standing about a metre away from what looks a bit like a thin wardrobe when it's closed up.

"It's...it's a bit of a surprise piece of furniture, I suppose," I say, my mouth dry. "It turns from this, into..."

I twist the wooden catch to release the vertical piece; support it down; crouch to fix its leg into place.

"...a table."

"Right," he says again but on an upward note this time. He steps closer.

He runs his hand over the surface of the table, tracing around the grain in the middle, which I took particular care over. I actually managed to find and adjoin two symmetrical boards from Querky's heart wood.

Then he gazes at the upright, dominated by the pine picture frame and in it, vastly enlarged, the photo of Mont Blanc and the Alps I took that day for Sab, its blues and whites shining out from the soft tones of the oak frame.

Grandad turns to me, his eyes gleaming.

"And you made all this, Sunshine?"

I nod, smiling. "It's adapted from a shepherd's table. For rooms short on space. Only I'm calling it a miner's table. It's for you, for your new kitchen. If you want it. I've designed it so it'll fit against that short wall."

"For me?" he repeats, still taking everything in.

"Yep, and you're the first person to see it too."

"And *you* did all this," he repeats to himself, a statement of…wonder, actually!

I finally start to relax.

"Haven't you guessed, Grandad?"

"What?"

I show him the photos I've mounted and stuck on the garage wall of all the stages of the process from our living oak to the table, watching my precious grandad to witness the second when it dawns.

"It never is, is it?"

I nod, this mad smile across my cheeks.

"But we sent Querky to Hackspace, Niv," he says, his hand resting on the table.

"We did. But then…"

I show him the whole process via the storyboard I've made, showing the stages: the how, when and where of reuniting him with our oak.

"This really is our tree, Niv," he tells me, his eyes brimming as he strokes the tabletop again, so gently.

Teary but smiley at the same time, I go on to show him the photo of the shepherd's table from Chalet Ouzon to show it's originally an Alpine idea.

"The picture frame, though, that's my adaptation," I tell him. "The point is, you can change it whenever you want—your window on the world."

"This view's just perfect," he says, turning to admire it again.

Now he runs his hands down the vertical sides of the upright, shaking his head. "There's some hours of work in this, lass, I'll say." He looks at me now. "It's a right bobby dazzler."

My throat tightens. That makes it all worthwhile.

"Can I?" I ask, my phone poised, and I snap a photo of my grandad standing next to his beloved friend, giving me the happiest smile I've seen for many months.

A face peers in at the door. "Ready?" Claude asks.

"What next?" Grandad asks, bewildered.

While Claude holds open the door, Mum and Dominique carefully carry in the hostess trolley between them, both shelves laden with sandwiches, samosas, sausage rolls, cakes and scones. Sab follows them in with a jug of milk and a big bottle of water.

"Well, I'll go t' bottom of our garden!" Grandad says as Mum rolls the food nearer to the table.

"No, ours!" I say and we all burst out laughing.

"Come and see what our Niv's done," Grandad says.

I demonstrate the table folding up and down to everyone else, though Claude's got to learn not to get in the way of it being lowered or else it'll brain him.

"You did it, Niv!" Mum says, putting her arm around me.

"Just!" I was still fitting the picture frame yesterday, after school. "And I'd never have done it without you," I tell Sab. "Owe you, big time."

"You'll do the same for me, one day, eh? Just not the hauling wood around thing, obvs!"

While Mum transfers the food from the trolley to the miner's table, I set out the folding chairs we keep in the garage roughly around it. Dominique puts on the kettle I brought down earlier and arranged on one of the garage shelves, along with tea, coffee and spoons.

"All ready?" I ask Mum.

"Almost," she says, putting her phone away. "But you've forgotten someone."

"Of course—we can't have a party without Rova!"

As I SKIP up the stepping-stone pavings to the kitchen, the sun finally breaks through, and I scoot along the hallway, about to call Rova out from the front room when the doorbell rings. I hesitate—I want to get back to Grandad and our party!—but it buzzes again, longer this time.

Sighing, I stride to the door. It could be a delivery, I s'pose. In fact, Mum's been asking me recently about the tools I most need. I open the door, half-hoping to find a large cardboard box.

It's not a box the hands are holding, though. It's a square contour map. Of the Alps.

"But..." I say, my eyes tracking upwards.

"I've brought the mountains to you," Jean-Lou says.

"Ooh!" I say, joy bursting in my chest as I throw myself into his arms.

"You even smell of the mountains, Jean-Lou," I tell him, eventually forcing myself away. "But what are you doing here?"

We shouldn't have been seeing each other for another three weeks, at half-term, in Drouzin, starting with the official opening of L'Igloo, visiting Miska's puppies, then some days at Chalet Ouzon.

"I was invited to a party!"

"Mum? I can't believe it!" I squeak in English. She must have known he was arriving now! "Come in, come in!"

I pull him inside, and he hands the mountains to me as he shrugs off his backpack.

Singing inside, I'm in a whirl. Is this really happening? Jean-Lou is here? In my hallway? Now?

Suddenly Rova appears between us, having nosed the door open! Jean-Lou sinks to his knees and rubs her between the ears.

"*Salut, chérie,*" he murmurs to her.

"Hey! You never called me darling!" I tell him, mock-cross.

"How could I ever call you anything better than Nirvana?" He looks up at me, his eyes warm.

Rova turns her head into his hand, then rests her long nose on his shoulder before turning to lick his cheek.

"Paws off, Rova!" I tell her in English. "He's mine!"

Jean-Lou straightens up. "Don't worry, Nirvana," he says, his dimple appearing as he catches the gist, "I would far prefer to kiss you."

We're together, his kiss tells me, *celebrating. All's well.*

We knew in our igloo we had a responsibility not to rip ourselves away from each other just because of inconvenient geography. We were in tears even at the thought of it!

"How long are you here for?" I whisper.

His face lights up. "Till tomorrow evening—a whole bonus thirty-six hours!"

I beam. "Come and meet everyone else."

"One second," he says, unzipping his backpack and drawing out two tubs. "Papa has sent some cheeses and some Savoie biscuits."

As we walk through the house, Rova trailing after Jean-Lou, I have to keep stopping and grabbing some part of him. "I can't believe you're here!"

Once we get into the garden, Claude comes galloping towards us.

"You're here!" he yells in French.

He stops short in front of Jean-Lou, twice his height. I've never, literally never, seen Claude shy before.

"*Salut*, Claude," Jean-Lou says, bending his knees and holding out his hand.

"*Salut*," he says, holding up his little one. "Have you been skiing this week, Jean-Louis?"

"I'm not keen on skiing," Jean-Lou tells him.

Scandalised, Claude's eyes widen.

"I do like to ride with husky dogs, though," Jean-Lou tells him. "I'll show you some photos when I've met everyone else."

"After that, we'll play Labyrinth," Claude tells him.

Jean-Lou turns to smile at me.

"What's that, Niv?" Claude asks me, noticing the relief map still in my hand.

Jean-Lou crouches down to get him to point out where Lac Leman is, the Ouzon mountains, Mont Blanc.

We walk towards the garage, Claude firing questions at Jean-Lou, Rova still at his side.

WHEN WE REACH the door, Claude grabs the mountains off me to go and show Grandad where we spent Christmas. Jean-Lou and I pause, taking in the other four chatting away around our table.

Mum comes first to welcome Jean-Lou.

"Surprised, Niv?" she asks, smiling at me.

"Totally!" I tell her, giving her a quick hug. I shake my head at Jean-Lou. "*And* he's been messaging me this morning as if he was in France! Thank you so much, Mum!"

Then I introduce him to Dominique. As they speak in fast French, I can see her weighing him up. On my account, I suspect.

Although they've obviously noticed his arrival, Sab and Grandad have stayed sitting around the table. I catch snatches of her telling him about the role Alz and his van played in Querky's transformation.

"Let me introduce you to my father, Jean-Louis," Mum says. "Perhaps Nirvana has told you, he does not speak French."

Grandad struggles up from the low chair to meet him and gives him a long look.

"So then," he says, "this is our Niv's young man, is it?"

My face burns, though I'm struggling to find other ways of describing what Jean-Lou is to me, and I quite like the phrase. I'm guessing Mum's filled Grandad in about his arrival while I've been inside.

"Well, I'm right glad to meet you," Grandad tells him, shaking his hand.

"I am pleased to meet you also," Jean-Lou says in his best English accent.

"I gather I have you to thank for th'idea for this 'ere table," Grandad says.

Knowing Jean-Lou'll be lost now, I step in to translate while Jean-Lou gives the mountain photo a closer look before running his palm around the edge of the tabletop.

"*Bravo, ma petite druide!*" he says as he puts his arm around my waist. "I knew from the start you'd do it."

"You were the only one who did then!"

"Tea?" Grandad offers a mug to Jean-Lou.

"He only drinks coffee, thanks, Grandad," I tell him.

I'll make him an espresso in Dominique's machine—when I can drag myself away.

Sab comes across with some plates.

"Jean-Louis, Sab," I say, dead proud to have my two friends together.

"*Enchanté,*" he tells her.

"Me too," she says, smiling. "Hungry, Jean-Louis?" She holds out a plate.

"Always," he says in English, grinning as he takes it from her.

When he turns to fill his plate from the food trolley, Sab flicks a glance at me. *Enchanté? Dimple?* her eyes say in mock disbelief.

I STEP AWAY to take some more photos on my phone. *How has this even happened?* I gaze at everyone I love clustered around the miner's table. Querky's wood glowing; it's gradually becoming populated by plates and mugs, as it should be. This table, made by me for my grandad from his beloved tree, inspired by Jean-Lou and made possible by Sab. With a lot of help from my friends, I did what I set out to do. I don't yet know whether it'll earn me the apprenticeship I want at Winslow Wood, but I have at least got an interview next Thursday.

I smile to myself at Sab and Jean-Lou having to make comical hand signals to try to compensate for his few English phrases and her dreadful French. Mum and Grandad are trying to reason with Claude about why feeding Rova samosas is not the best idea.

My eyes shift back to the table, the mountains now sitting in the middle. I love the link it forms between Jean-Lou's grandparents and my Grandad, the bringing of the Alps into deepest Lancashire!

Dominique's leaning against the garage wall next to it and catches my eye. Indicating Jean-Lou with a tiny tilt of her head, she mouths a message to me.

Top, Nirvan-ah!

I beam at her. These very different people, different from each other, different from me, coming together for a little party in a garage. I still don't know all the answers about what brings people close. I think back to Jean-Lou's definition of chemistry as the way elements connect to create change. He and I bonded like two unstable atoms. In the Alps, an igloo and L'Igloo; here in Lancashire, a unique table and this unlikely group; all new and lovely things created as a result of our meeting on Christmas Eve.

Jean-Lou looks across at me now, his dimple a tick at the end of his very happiest mouth.

I smile back.

No more hiding away.

ABOUT THE AUTHOR

Just like Nirvana, Jennifer grew up in Lancashire. Also like Nirvana, she loves mountains, Christmas and border collies! The village where Nirvana met Jean-Louis is based on the one where Jennifer and her family used to own a little chalet, in Haute Savoie. There the similarities end, unfortunately.

Jennifer taught English, Drama and Classics for twenty years in several schools, including four years in Paris. She later completed an MA in Creative Writing for Children at Manchester Metropolitan University and is also an alumna of the Golden Egg Academy.

Now retired, at least from teaching, Jennifer lives with her husband in West Yorkshire but enjoys travelling to new places, particularly if they have mountains, including most recently to beautiful Romania. *Igloo* is her debut novel; her work-in-progress is *Going West*, a story for adults.

Website: https://www.jennifer-burkinshaw.com

ACKNOWLEDGEMENTS

Many have expressed this better with metaphors, but more prosaically, shaping a novel into the best version of itself is a long, hard slog, wholly impossible without lots of help.

My thanks are chronological through my journey as a writer so far, beginning with Imogen Cooper at the Golden Egg Academy who, over several years' mentoring, really helped me to develop my craft on my MA novel, *Happiness Seekers*, also for young adults. In terms of *Igloo* specifically, I'm immensely grateful to Tilda Johnson, also part of the GEA, who faithfully saw me through several drafts editorially, including when the pandemic struck just as *Igloo* was 'ready'. The market changed, and *Igloo* needed to shift into the Christmas romance it has ended up being.

Thank you too to my highly talented critique group, NW SCBWI, many of whom have read various submissions of *Igloo* over several years and incarnations! I can't name them all, but I must thank Eve Chancellor for often reading extra/longer extracts, often at short notice, and always being prepared to talk through characters and plot points by text or phone. Thank you, Eve, for always being so willing and for being such a champion of Niv; special thanks also to Ruth Estevez, Louisa Reid, Anna Mainwaring and Helen Lapping for always being supportive of my writing and giving me the benefit of their experience.

For help and suggestions with those all-important first chapters, I'm very grateful to Adam Green and Bryony Pearce. Sincere thanks to my very dear friends Julie Davis and Hilary Dixon, for reading, listening and encouraging.

Heartfelt thanks to my sister-in-law, Liz Burkinshaw, and niece, Charlotte Burkinshaw for giving up one of the hottest days of the year to make trailers for *Igloo*. Thank you, Liz, for your technical and photography skills, creativity and ongoing patience with me. And Charlotte, thank you for 'being' Nirvana and being prepared to put on a ski jacket and woolly hat in 36°C to appear in a cardboard igloo, amongst many other things!

Lastly, in this whole process of *Igloo* actually reaching readers, is the one wonderful woman who has joined up the circle that started with the very first draft by offering to publish it. Debbie McGowan, in itself that would be enough to make you my absolute hero, but to add to all that, you're a person of total integrity, huge intelligence, wide-ranging abilities and immense kindness. How lucky am I to be part of your Beaten Track team!